A Timely Murder

Pet Psychic Cozy Mysteries

Max Parrott

Copyright © 2020 by Max Parrott

All rights reserved.

No portion of this book may be reproduced in any form without written permission from the publisher or author, except as permitted by U.S. copyright law.

Contents

Chapter 1 — 1
Chapter 2 — 6
Chapter 3 — 12
Chapter 4 — 17
Chapter 5 — 24
Chapter 6 — 30
Chapter 7 — 37
Chapter 8 — 46
Chapter 9 — 49
Chapter 10 — 56
Chapter 11 — 63
Chapter 12 — 71
Chapter 13 — 79
Chapter 14 — 85
Chapter 15 — 91
Chapter 16 — 98
Chapter 17 — 105
Chapter 18 — 114
Chapter 19 — 120

Chapter 20	124
Chapter 21	133
Chapter 22	136

Chapter 1

"What a difference from Blackwood Cove!"

Jasmine smiled as she jogged along, pulled by her enthusiastic friend. Luffy was correct in his observation. While their hometown was cold and clammy and gray, this place was green and bright and full of life. Blackwood Cove, even in summer time, was possessed of a certain leaden weight, as though the heart of winter resided somewhere deep in the ground beneath it and bled its influence into the town all year round.

Together, the two friends raced down a wide asphalt path. To their right was a guardrail and a two-lane road, the main line that stretched between New Market and Wildwood College. To their left was nothing but forest, an untouched and unmapped vastness where the wild spirit of the old frontier still seemed to exist. Ancient trees brooded tall and heavy over everything else, filling the understory with shadow and calm and silence. A chipmunk chittered; a car ambled by at forty miles an hour, its tires a whisper on the surface of the road.

Luffy looked back, his tongue hanging out of his mouth. "Pretty dang hot out here for a Spring day!"

"Getting tired on me?" Jasmine asked between breaths, grinning as sweat streamed over her forehead and upper lip. She reached up and wiped it out of her eyes, looking at the brand-new GPS watch her father had sent her as a birthday gift. Four and a half miles in. Nearly there.

The journey from her apartment at the edge of New Market to the school was six miles. And a lot could change over that distance. Civilization became wilderness. The hustle and bustle of a large town was reduced to the faint buzzing of insects and the trilling of birds as they swept to and fro on their unknown missions.

This was the middle of Jasmine's first semester at school. Wildwood was not a cheap school, and to make ends meet she had foregone the purchase of a car. She had a bicycle, but she rarely used it.

"Tired?" Luffy asked. "Never. I could run all day, you know that. How about you, huh? Can you keep up?"

She answered him with action rather than words, picking up her pace and blowing right past. He leapt to keep up, and did so easily. With four legs, the eight-minute pace Jasmine usually went at was nothing to him.

Twelve minutes later, the path began to drift away from the road and wind into the forest itself. At first this seemed like a pointless meandering, but suddenly the forest opened into a vista of the college. It sat on fifty acres of cleared space and took up only half of that, leaving the rest as sports fields, walking trails and empty expanses of grass where students and staff often had their lunch.

Wildwood was a symmetrical grouping of granite buildings that had stood here for close to two hundred years. Minor renovations had been done, electricity, water and telephone added and then, much later, internet, but it existed pretty much as it did when it was first built. The asphalt path transferred into ancient flagstone pavers as Jaz and Luffy crossed the threshold of the school grounds. They slowed down, walking the rest of the way, both craning their necks to survey the looming school. Because of the forest surrounding it, much of

Wildwood stood in deep shadow at this early hour. All but the clock tower, which rose up into the sun, its face blazing like a beacon.

"It's quite a sight, huh?" Luffy asked.

Jasmine nodded. In a moment they were surrounded by other students, lounging on the grass and studying for whatever class they were about to go into. Only a few of them looked up at Luffy in surprise; most were already used to the dog's presence here.

The two friends circled around the back of the building and approached a smaller structure that stood a short distance away from the main cluster. It used to be a carriage house or some such thing, but it had, sometime in the first half of the last century, been retrofitted as a gymnasium. Wildwood did not have a large athletics program. In fact, the only two programs it offered were track and field and wrestling. But it had a long history of excellence, and part of keeping the mind sharp lay in training the body. It was one of the tenets of the college, and every student was encouraged to use the gym any hour, any day.

Jasmine had taken that encouragement and ran with it. She and Luffy entered the building and skirted around a pilates class that was already underway. They went into the locker room. Jasmine approached a bench and lowered her heavy backpack onto it. From inside she pulled out a change of clothes and a metal bowl. The latter she filled with water and left on the floor for Luffy. The former she took with her into a shower stall to wash off the stench of the run. She used her hands to scrub sunscreen from her face and arms.

While she was in the middle of washing, she heard someone else enter the locker room. The newcomer began talking to Luffy, no doubt scratching his ears and rubbing his belly and all the other things the Golden Retriever liked.

Jasmine shut off the water and patted herself dry. She was still self-conscious about wandering around the locker room with nothing but a towel to cover herself, so she quickly dressed inside the stall and stepped out to find a familiar young woman giving Luffy his very own massage treatment.

"You big ham," she said, shaking her head.

Luffy let out a groan of contentment. "Being a dog does have its advantages."

Alicia Newman looked up, smiling. "Luffy's a good boy. Aren't you Luffy?"

"Sheesh," he said, still smiling. "And that's one of the disadvantages. People think they need to talk to you like you're a baby."

Jasmine smiled, lowering herself onto the bench to put her shoes back on.

"He likes you," she said.

Alicia shrugged. "Dogs like everyone."

Jasmine shook her head. "Not true. I know someone who Luffy doesn't like at all."

"Oh? Who?"

"Just someone from back home," Jasmine replied. "What brings you in here, anyway? Are you in that pilates class?"

"Me? God, no," Alicia said, laughing. "I'm about as flexible as a steel rod. I'm pretty sure I'd snap in half if I tried doing any of that stuff. I just saw you heading this way so I thought I'd stop by."

Jasmine grinned. "You didn't do the homework, did you?"

"Well..." Alicia returned the grin, looking sheepish. "It was either that, or get the four hours of sleep I managed to get."

"Did you ever think about, I dunno, taking less of a workload?"

Alicia nodded. "Next semester. I just don't want to be in school forever, you know? So, are you gonna help me out?"

Jasmine sighed, reaching for her bag. "You owe me."

"I still owe you for last time," Alicia said.

"Okay. So you owe me double."

She pulled out her worksheets. But rather than simply give Alicia the answers, she tried to be as instructional as possible. There was no point in cheating if you were going to come away from it just as ignorant as before.

"So, let me get this straight," Alicia said at the end. "A weird teenager and a scared old man were really all it took for this guy to completely change his mind? It was enough to make him see how screwed up the world is?"

"No!" Jasmine said, laughing. "There's more to it than that. You just need to actually read the book."

"I will, I promise," said Alicia. "This weekend. But I just need to get through this class. Please, Jasmine."

She shook her head firmly. "You've gotten all the help you're going to get from me."

"Not fair. You've probably already read the book five times."

"I admit nothing," Jasmine replied with a smile.

Alicia gave her a playful slap on the arm. "Well, if I fail it's all your fault."

"You won't fail. You're smart enough. College is half knowing the answers and half knowing how to stumble into them. Right?"

"Something like that." Alicia looked at the time on her phone. "Crap! We'd better go."

Luffy jumped up. "Are we running again? Let's go!"

Chapter 2

Professor Hawke's Creative Writing class was one of the largest at Wildwood, at least in terms of size. However this semester a record low number of students had elected to take it. So Jasmine and the others stepped into a rather empty and deserted lecture hall. The majority of the desks were still covered in cloth from the winter break; half the lights in the ceiling were turned off, leaving a small semicircle of illumination around the professor's desk and blackboard.

Jasmine took her seat near the middle of the existing class. Luffy obediently slinked in under the desk, lying down and breathing out the rest of the heat he had generated on the run.

Despite Alicia's concerns, they were some of the first people to arrive. As the students trickled in at a slow pace, it became clear that a few desks would remain empty. Jasmine felt herself wondering if the desk directly in front of her would be one of those... but a minute before the bell, Charles Dane came strolling in as though he was on a relaxing walk through the park.

Tall and well dressed, with hair that was never less than perfectly coiffed, Charles was the definition of a preppy. His expression seemed to flip between a self-satisfied smirk and a grimace of disgust, and nothing else. He appraised Jasmine as he reached his seat, huffing a bit when he saw Luffy lounging in the shadows beneath the desk.

"Still allowed to bring that beast in here?" Charles asked. "I swear his breath is worse than my grandfather's, and he's dead."

"Newsflash," Luffy said. "Those are my farts you've been smelling. Enjoy."

Despite his words, Charles reached back as he sat down and very stealthily gave the dog a pat on the head. He wasn't all bad, just mostly. As Alicia sometimes liked to say.

"So, what is it today?" Charles sighed, opening his bag. "More of that insufferable sci-fi nonsense? I thought this class was for literature."

"Science fiction is one of the greatest kinds of literature," Jasmine said in response.

"Yes?" Charles asked, glancing back, his expression seemingly balanced between the two extremes he was known for. "How so?"

"It reflects on human nature in ways that no other genre can, because it shows us events that could happen but haven't yet. It draws parallels with history and shows us how the world might look in the future."

Charles shrugged. "It's all a lot of nonsense. Pulp writers who somehow got lucky enough to get their own section at the bookstore. Nothing more."

"What is that I hear?" called a shrill voice from the front of the class.

Until now, Professor Sampson Hawke had been sitting quite still and peacefully. Now he stood from his desk, lifting his ever-present mug of tea and approaching the first row of seats. He reached up to adjust his small glasses but somehow they stayed perched at the very end of his nose.

"Class technically hasn't started yet," Professor Hawke added. "But..."

He glanced at his watch.

"...now it has," he added. "I see that some of our more enthusiastic students may have an opinion to share. Charles, Jasmine, is there anything you'd like to say to the rest of the class? Any discussion or debate you'd like to start?"

As always with Professor Hawke, it was difficult to tell whether he was being genuine or else seeking some sort of disciplinary action.

The rest of the students looked around, shifting in their seats.

"Uh, no sir," Charles said. "We were just discussing how we got on with last night's homework."

"Right," Jasmine said.

The professor nodded. "I see. I could have sworn I heard someone insulting one of the most beautiful branches of fiction to be found, but I guess that doesn't matter. Everyone's entitled to their opinion."

He turned back to the blackboard. With the hand he wasn't using to hold his cup of tea, he grabbed a bit of chalk and scrawled something out on the board.

Method and Means of Writing.

Then he turned to the class.

"By now you all should have finished reading Fahrenheit 451," he said. "And you also should have reached the afterword, though I'm sure many of you didn't bother to read it. Basically, half of the idea for the novel started out as a short story based on a real-life experience. The original story was only like the resulting novel in tertiary ways. Any writer could have been inspired to write a novel based on it, and the resulting novels would all differ vastly. The fact that Mr. Bradbury came up with Fahrenheit 451 speaks to his own individual method of writing."

He used the chalk to point at the first word he had written.

"The method refers to the exact words and how they are ordered. How they make up the story, the characters, the morals and purpose of the whole thing. Mr. Bradbury used his poetic and greatly analogistic style of writing to give us an unforgettable and singular work. That is his method. But what about the means?

"The means refers to the physical way in which a thing is written. Dalton Trumbo used to like to write longhand from his bathtub. Roald Dahl had a favorite armchair he liked to tuck himself away in with his legs in a sleeping bag. To bring up another giant of science fiction, Isaac Asimov enjoyed shutting himself in tight, closed spaces to hammer away at his typewriter and then his word processor with superhuman speed. Ray Bradbury, in writing Fahrenheit 451, came to a method that was not normal for him.

"Rather than write at home, where he would be distracted, he sought a quieter place to work. But he couldn't afford office space, so he elected to write on a typewriter in the basement of a library. A typewriter he had to pay to operate. All in all the novel took him eighteen days to write and cost somewhere close to twenty dollars. That was not Bradbury's preferred method of writing, but it was the method he used. The result was a beautiful and lasting novel that we read to this very day."

Charles shifted slightly in his seat, probably just seeking a more comfortable position.

"Oh, I'm sorry Mr. Dane," Professor Hawke snapped. "Am I boring you, or offending your literary sensibilities? I apologize. Perhaps next time we can cover the works of Lord Byron or Shakespeare. Or maybe you would prefer George Eliot? For now, let's talk about how creativity is the key term in the phrase 'creative writing,' and how the means of writing can change while the methods stay the same..."

"Is it just me," Alicia said, "or did Professor Hawke seem snippier today?" "I'll say," Charles said with a sigh. "I thought he was going to crawl down my throat at one point. The man's on a tear."

They were walking to their next class, a language and linguistics course which they happened to share. Luffy strolled along beside them, drawing a disapproving stare from a passing custodian.

"He was fine yesterday," Jasmine pointed out. "Something must be bothering him."

"Well, he'd better sort it out," said Charles. "If this abuse keeps up, I'll have no choice but to let my father know."

Alicia laughed. "Really? You'll let your father know?"

Charles shrugged. "Why not?"

"Because it'll turn you into a walking, talking cliché," Alicia replied.

"Too late," said Luffy.

Jasmine cracked up laughing. Alicia grinned, assuming it was at her own remark.

Charles scowled at both of them. "Why am I friends with the two of you, anyway?"

"Because we're awesome," Jasmine said.

"Keep thinking that," Charles grumbled.

"What's with you, anyway?" Jasmine asked. "I'm used to you having a silver spoon up your butt, but today it's like there's a whole telephone pole up there."

Charles went stiff, his usual languid walking gait transmuting into something upright but shambling. Like an undead butler.

"Don't worry about him," Alicia said, giving Jasmine a nudge. "He's just upset about not getting that position on the student council."

"What a shambles," Charles griped. "What a miscarriage of responsibility and duty. Everyone knows I should have had that position. Everyone."

"Just let your dad know," said Alicia. "He'll figure it out for you."

Charles scoffed. "Contrary to your inexplicably negative opinion of me, I don't require my father's assistance with every last matter that pops up. I'm going to take care of this one myself."

"Yeah?" Luffy asked, looking back with his tongue hanging out. "How are you going to swing that one, chief?"

Charles answered without needing a transposition from Luffy's human companion.

"I'm going to speak with Dean DuPont and see if we can't sort this out," he said. "In this and in all matters, logic should prevail. It will become clear that I am a much better candidate for the position than that pauper."

Jasmine had no idea which muckraker he was referring to. She had enough on her plate, reading two or three novels a week and writing her own short stories and novellas, that she didn't pay a whole lot of attention to school politics. It was all quite dry to her, far less interesting than the imagined worlds contained in all the pages of the school library, a room that was rivaled only by The Book Nook in its ability to capture her.

By then the four of them were approaching their next class. Technically it was called Language and Linguistics: How Our Words and the Way We Use Them Influence Our Understanding of the World, but for obvious reasons it was often called LnL for short, even by its professor.

Where Professor Hawke was eccentric, moody, and prone to sudden outbursts, Professor Alan Keller was a quiet and brooding man who seemed to both hate and love the English language in equal measure. His hair grew in two stages. At the sides it came in as wild tufts, and on top as faint wisps on his liver-spotted scalp. What he lacked up top he made up for down below, with a Shakespearean beard and mustache that put the old Bard to shame in its dimensions and style.

Professor Keller was in his usual posture as the students filtered in, reclining in the wing-backed monstrosity he used in place of a normal desk chair, his feet up on an ancient, threadbare ottoman and a razor thin, modern laptop perched on his skinny legs. His legs were crossed at the ankles, and he seemed to be as comfortable as any man had ever managed to get. There was a small microphone taped to his lapel; a huge profusion of notes had already been written out on the board, starting with numbered instructions which the students followed. They sat and, in near silence, took out their books and turned to the right page.

"Another note taking session," Charles complained. "When are we actually going to learn something in this class?"

It was that moment when another young man, sitting in the very next row, looked back and gave Charles a friendly smile. Jasmine had seen this boy around. He seemed nice. She thought his name was Oliver. But the sight of him seemed to have an effect on Charles that was similar to that of being immersed in a vat of cold slime. He shivered from head to toe, and made a disgusted noise.

"That rat," he said as he took his seat. "That absolute waste of skin!"

"What's wrong with him?" Jasmine asked.

Alicia leaned over. "That's Oliver Bridges, the one who took the position Charles was after."

Jasmine shrugged. Obviously it would be annoying to lose out on a position you wanted, but Charles's reaction seemed quite over the top. Then again, everything about Charles seemed over the top. She put it out of her mind and refocused her attention on the front of the room as Dr. Keller cleared his throat and began the lecture from the comfort of his armchair.

"It may not seem like it," he said. "But language is both the finest tool and the deadliest weapon available to us. It can cause unimagined destruction and bountiful growth, depending on mere inflection..."

"Oh, we'll find out about the power of language," Charles grumbled. "We'll find out very soon."

Chapter 3

Jasmine entered the dining hall having forgotten all about Charles and his anger. She hadn't eaten since the banana she quickly scarfed that morning before leaving on her six-mile run. And neither had Luffy. Right now, her dog and her stomach were both competing to see who could be the loudest and the most annoying.

"I'm wasting away to nothing, here!" Luffy said. "What are you standing around for? Let's go eat! Smells like chicken! Oh, there's some pizza!"

As they made their way through the hall, Luffy darted slightly from side to side, thrusting his nose in the air to get a whiff off everyone's tray as he passed. He was drooling by the time they reached the food line.

"I swear, Jasmine," he said. "If you get me plain ground beef and a hardboiled egg again, I'll pee on your favorite running shoes."

Jasmine chuckled, grabbing a tray and then pulling the food bowl out of her pack. "Don't worry. Today's a special treat!"

"Well, maybe you can give me the egg," Luffy added.

"What, and smell your farts all night again?" Jasmine asked, lowering her voice so no one would hear her over the hum of the crowd.

"Yeah, they are pretty bad," Luffy said. "If you give me two, I think I'll be able to make Charles run out of class tomorrow."

"Shh," Jasmine warned. "You're lucky I don't just give you kibble."

She piled her tray with all the healthiest option she could find. Steamed fish, broccoli, a salad loaded with greens. Then, just for balance, she threw on a bread roll and a small piece of cake. Much to Luffy's disappointment, it was chocolate and thus he would not be allowed to lick the frosting off her fork after.

It was true, Jasmine thought, that she had friends. She and Alicia always sat close to each other in classes they shared. And Charles, as insufferable as he could be, was inexplicably interesting to her. She liked having him around, for his entertaining anecdotes and outbursts if for no other reason.

But these things did not obligate her to sit at any one dining table. She often wandered around, picking spots at random. Sometimes she would sit alone, or near to some person she had never met.

Today, as she was walking along with Luffy nearby, his eyes glued to the food tray and his tongue moving incessantly over his chops, she spotted Oliver. At first she didn't recognize him in his reading glasses. And she almost missed him entirely, for he was nearly obscured by the huge thick book that was propped on the table in front of him. Every few moment his hand would wander idly to the side. Without looking, and with mixed success, he would stab a bite of food and bring it toward his mouth. His eyes never seemed to leave the page.

As Jasmine approached him, her legs carrying her automatically, she bent her head slightly to read the title of the book on the spine. It was Critique of Pure Reason by Immanuel Kant. She had heard of the writer himself, but had not come across a single volume of his work in all her years.

"Philosophy?" she asked, taking the seat across from him and plunking down her food tray. She lifted Luffy's bowl to the floor and, without complaint, he dug into the carrots and shredded chicken she had provided.

For a long moment silence reigned at the table. Other than the chomping, slurping, swallowing sounds from below, nothing happened. The wall of the book remained upright. The only thing that seemed to change was the color of the fingers gripping it on either side. They went from olive-tanned to white as their grip tightened.

Finally, like a cautious turtle, Oliver stretched up his seat to glance at her over the top of the tome. He was wearing a small, awkward smile.

"Yes," he said simply, before sinking back down.

"Is that what you're studying?" Jasmine asked.

"Yes," he replied, this time without bothering to look at her.

"Cool. There weren't many philosophy books where I came from. Mostly just novels and self-help books."

"Huh," Oliver said.

Luffy paused from wolfing down his lunch to glance up at her. "Why don't you leave the kid alone? Obviously he doesn't want to be bothered with a book that size sitting in front of him!"

Ordinarily, Jasmine would have agreed. She didn't know why she was here, or why she was asking these questions, just like she didn't know why her legs had decided to carry her this way without a single approval from her mind. It seemed right. It seemed like the thing to do. And over the past few months, she had learned to trust her feelings.

"Would you mind reading to me a little bit?" she asked.

The head came up again. Oliver grinned at her, looking embarrassed.

"I don't know," he said.

"Just a short little bit. I'm curious."

"Well..." His head sunk back down, and he cleared his throat before continuing. "'Now on this persistence there is also grounded a correction of the concept of alteration. Arising and perishing are not alterations of that which arises or perishes. Alteration is a way of existing that succeeds another way of existing of the very same object. Hence everything that is altered is lasting, and only its state changes.'"

"Was that even English?" Luffy asked.

"Huh," Jasmine said in return. "I guess now I know why I didn't go in for philosophy."

Oliver seemed to shrug from behind his literary wall. "It's simpler than it sounds. You're missing the whole context."

Jasmine nodded. "I guess it sounds like he's just trying to say that stuff never goes away. It just changes."

"That is an interpretation," said Oliver.

"So, if you die, you aren't actually gone. You're just in a different state."

"I suppose," he replied.

Jasmine laughed. "That's a long book. Are you reading it for class or just enjoyment?"

Finally, Oliver gave up and laid the book down on its back. His face was revealed, along with the stains on his shirt where his fumbling method of eating was apparent.

"For class, obviously," he said. "We don't even have to read the whole thing, just selected parts. But I thought it would be better if I went through all of it. And it isn't as long as it looks. The first quarter of the dang thing is just introductions and prefaces."

"Did you bother reading those?"

"No. No one does. So what are you in for?" he asked.

"Murder," Jasmine said without hesitation, letting her eyes go wide and crazy.

Oliver chuckled, averting his gaze. "Oh... um, I see."

"But that's just my minor," Jasmine went on. "I'm here for an English degree. Yeah, I know what you're going to say. The same thing my aunt used to ask me. What in the world are you going to do with an English degree, wash dishes?"

"Well, what are you going to do?" Oliver asked.

"Follow my dreams. The same thing everyone should do. I want to be the editor of my own magazine one day. Maybe I'm just picky, but I think half the stuff that gets published is kind of..."

"Crap?" Oliver offered.

She laughed. "Maybe. I just think I'd like to throw my hat in the ring, publish the kind of stuff I really like to read. I think it would be cool."

Oliver nodded. "Yeah, that actually does sound pretty cool."

He shifted a bit in his seat, looking uncomfortable. Jasmine knew the posture well. He had something he wanted to say or ask, but was either too shy or too embarrassed to come out with it.

"Go on," she said.

"Well... I was kind of surprised when I saw you in LnL at the start of the semester. I thought someone like you might, I dunno, try and get into law enforcement. We don't really have any programs like that at Wildwood."

"So, you know all about that stuff, huh?" Jasmine asked.

Oliver shrugged. "I think pretty much everyone does. Maybe you could have flown under the radar if it was just you. But..."

He gestured under the table.

"Huh?" Luffy said, lifting his head from his nearly empty dish. "You got a treat for me?"

Jasmine laughed. "He does kind of give it away, doesn't he?"

"I think it's cool that you're here," Oliver said quickly. "I was just surprised, that's all."

"Don't worry about it. All that stuff... it was just something I kind of fell into. It felt like something I needed to do at the time. And then, there was that rest area by the state line. That was kind of a fluke. Bad luck, or good luck, or whatever you want to call it. I don't really plan on making a life out of solving murders."

"Good," Oliver replied. "I was really hoping you wouldn't have to bust out your skills here at Wildwood. It's always been a safe place and, well... some people have been saying you're bad luck. Not me," he added, seeing her face. "Just some other idiots."

"Bad luck?" Luffy asked. "Tell me who said that and I'll go bite 'em! My girl Jasmine is the best luck anyone could ask for. She's got a one hundred percent success rate against murderers!"

"It's OK," Jasmine said, reaching down to scratch his ears. "People will say all kinds of things. Doesn't make them true."

Chapter 4

"You really ought to get your own car," Charles said. "I suppose you could probably afford something Japanese made. Or at least American. But my father says the upkeep on American cars is a killer. They end up in the shop for half the time you own them."

Jasmine shifted on the leather seat. She was in the back, holding Luffy between her knees. Keeping him still. She knew he would behave, and not scratch anything, but Charles insisted that he be sequestered. The dog looked up at Jasmine with misery in his eyes.

"Anyways, just a thought," said Charles, glancing in the mirror. "Not very talkative today, are we?"

"Just tired," Jasmine said. It was true. The run, followed by a string of mentally draining classes, had left her feeling like a helium balloon that had been run over; once light and buoyant, now flattened and crushed. To top it all off, she had a shift at work tonight. And an essay to finish.

"Unfortunately," Charles went on in his droning voice as he patted the dash of the car, "I'll probably have to let go of my baby soon. Father won't want to make the extra payments. My post-college career is now anything but assured."

Jasmine barely heard him. She was looking out the window at a familiar figure who was coming down the path toward the college. She didn't know who the man was. He was generally too old to be a student, and she never saw him in any classes, but he wasn't one of the school staff either. However, it was rare not to see him around the grounds of an early evening.

"So, what are your plans for the evening?" Charles asked. "I think I'll shut myself in my room and lie naked in front of a fan. When it's this hot in spring, you know you're in for a bad summer."

"I have to work," Jasmine replied. "And thanks for the visual."

"Any time. Work, did you say? I thought you had saved up enough?"

"For tuition," she said. "I've been saving up since I was little. All from the tooth fairy, birthday and Christmas money. But I still need to pay rent and utilities. My parents help out with half of it, but..."

"But New Market is not a cheap place to live," Charles replied.

He turned the steering wheel ever so slightly right. The finely tuned machine responded, magnifying his movement into a lovely curving turn. They coasted around a bend in the road, the tires sticking to the asphalt like they were covered in glue.

Six miles was quite far when you were on foot. But in a car, especially one driven by a young man from a wealthy family who was not worried about getting a speeding ticket, it was very fast indeed. Before they knew it they were sweeping out of the wilderness and into New Market, a town of almost twenty thousand people. She had heard both Charles and Alicia referring to it as "small," but neither of them had seen Blackwood Cove. Compared to her home town, Jasmine saw New Market as a sprawling metropolis.

Not that she had seen most of it. She lived neared the edge of town, and had her small segment she liked to stick to. There was a triangle in which she travelled; home, grocery store, work. Or perhaps the shape was more like a kite, and the string dangling off the bottom was the route she took to Wildwood. She kept meaning to get out and explore the town one of these days, but she just hadn't gotten around to it.

The first time Charles had given Jasmine a ride home, he had made fun of her choice in apartment. As if there was any choice at all. After seeing how much it hurt her, Charles had learned to shut up. A rare skill from him. The car was silent as they swept up the crumbling driveway of the apartment complex.

Lockwood Village, despite its fanciful name, was basically one step above a shanty town. Due to her refusal to have a roommate, Jasmine had no choice but to move in here. Luckily it was home to more ailing retirees than anything else. It was quiet. It was peaceful. And it was ugly as all get out. Smelly, too. Not that Luffy minded; the stink just gave him plenty of opportunities to mark his territory.

Charles pulled the car to a stop, looking around all antsy the way he always did. As though expected to be held up at gun point.

"Well," he said quickly. "Until next time."

Jasmine opened the door, letting Luffy jump out ahead of her before she climbed to her feet. "Thanks, Charles."

She shut the door, and watched him zoom away. He broke the speed limit once again in his haste to be out of here. Maybe he was afraid that every minute spent in Lockwood Village would cause another spot of rust to spontaneously appear on his "baby."

"I don't really like that guy," Luffy said. "Sure, he pets me sometimes, but…"

"He just doesn't understand, that's all," Jasmine replied. "Life hasn't given him a chance to understand."

She pulled her keys out of her pocket, and the jingling sound immediately stole Luffy's attention.

"Ooh, can we check the mail?" he asked, jumping up on his hind legs. "Can we, can we?"

"That's what I was going to do," she said with a smile.

They ventured through Lockwood Village together, passing cars that couldn't possibly be street legal and pickup trucks that surely wouldn't pass any recent emissions test. The mailboxes were as far from Jasmine's building as they could possibly be, a fact which had frustrated her as much as it excited Luffy.

Stepping along a crumbling asphalt drive past patches of overgrown weeds where playground equipment used to be, they finally reached the mailboxes. Jasmine opened her locker up and pulled out a handful of papers.

"Trash, trash, trash," she said, sorting through them as they started walking back. "Oh, look, coupons for a fast food place we don't even have in New Market. Makes sense! What a waste of paper."

"Has anyone ever told you that you complain too much?" Luffy asked.

"No, because it isn't true. I complain exactly the right amount. And what about you, huh? Last night you were whining thirty seconds after we came inside."

"I just had to pee all of a sudden," he replied. "You can't always predict that sort of thing, Jasmine. And there was a smell I wanted to check out too."

"Was it that dead raccoon by the dumpsters?" she asked.

"Could have been," he replied. "Who's to say? It's a mystery."

She laughed. "Maybe that should be our next case. Jaz and Luffy solve the mystery of the bloated animal corpse!"

"Come on, don't be ridiculous. No one would want to read that one."

Suddenly, Luffy's ears perked up and he turned back to face her. She felt it coming as well. She was getting better now, after being through enough of these episodes, at sensing them beforehand.

Looking both ways down the drive, she crossed quickly to the other side and let herself fall down in the shade of a pine tree. Needles crunched under her, poking her butt as she leaned against the sappy trunk and closed her eyes.

Luffy was there waiting when she opened them again a few seconds later. Unlike after her very first visions, she felt more lucid this time. There was none of the confusion, the dreamlike surreal feeling that had marked the first couple of experiences. She was back to reality in an instant, with the image as clear in her head as if she had just watched it on TV.

"Parking spaces," she said. "Something about parking spaces at Wildwood. That's all I saw."

"Talk about vague," said Luffy.

She shook her head. "They usually start off this way. They get more detailed as they go. I can't believe this is happening again. Can't I catch a break?"

Luffy whined nervously. "So you think someone's going to..."

"...end up dead?" she said, frowning. "I mean, what happened the last two times the visions happened?"

"Good point," said Luffy, his eyes shifting around nervously. "Let's get inside. Suddenly I don't feel very safe out here."

Jasmine used a tree branch to pull herself to her feet, smiling shakily. "Luffy doesn't want to be outside anymore? There's a first time for everything."

"Yeah, well, there's a first time for getting murdered too," Luffy said. "I'm sure you wouldn't be the first psychic to foresee your own death. I don't want that to happen."

Jasmine dusted herself off, collecting her mail and heading for home.

"I'm not psychic," she said.

"Yeah? And how do you explain the visions?"

She shrugged. "They just come to me. I don't seek them out. I don't even want them at all. Not right now. I've got too much other stuff to focus on."

"Maybe you're more like an antenna, right?" Luffy offered. "You catch incoming signals now and then. Little snippets. Doesn't mean you aren't psychic. You have visions, and you can talk to your dog."

Jasmine shrugged again. She didn't want to think about any of that. She had already thought about it for years, without finding an answer. She hadn't come to Wildwood to solve mysteries; she had come to prepare herself for a normal life.

But it seemed like the world might have other plans.

Jasmine climbed the outside stairs to the second level of her building and turned a corner at the top, readying her key to unlock the door.

But there was someone standing in her way, right outside her apartment. He was a small bearded man in his thirties. Scrawny, verging on malnourished, though he had filled out a bit since arriving in New Market. And he did not look very happy.

"Joe," she said with a sigh. "What are you doing here? I thought you had a place?"

He winced. "I had a bad day, Jasmine. A really bad day. I just wanted to..."

"It's okay, you don't have to say anything," she said, stepping past him to unlock her door. "I have to go to work in a little while, but you can come inside for now."

"Actually I was hoping I could... spend the night." She looked back at him. "You don't actually have a place, do you?" He shrugged.

"At least tell me you aren't sleeping inside a ceiling cavity again," she said.

"No!" he replied. "Nothing like that. I made a friend in town. He was letting me crash on his couch. But I guess his wife put her foot down."

Jasmine pushed the door open. "I guess you should find a single guy next time."

"I don't want to impose," Joe said. "It's just one night. I know people always say that, but I really mean it. I just had a bad day, that's all."

Jasmine nodded. "One night."

She stepped aside to let him enter, then shut the door. Joe stood around awkwardly as she went into the kitchen. She came back with two glasses of water and handed him one.

"You can sit down," she said.

Joe made his way to the recliner and sat gingerly, resting on the very edge of the seat. Jasmine sat on the floor where she could rub Luffy's belly.

"Is it anything you want to talk about?" she asked.

Joe shrugged. "Maybe. Not right now, though. I just wanted to see a familiar face. This town..."

"It's hard, I know. Suddenly you're thrust into this big, loud place full of strangers. It's not even easy for me."

He sighed. "I'm happy to hear you say that. I thought there was something wrong with me."

She shook her head. "You're perfectly sane, Joe. The world is just a crazy place. You'll figure it out. And if you're still struggling at the end of the semester, you can ride back to Blackwood Cove with me. It's a lot smaller. It might be easier for you. Maybe I could even hook you up with a job. The Sheriff there kind of owes me one."

"I don't think I could work at a police department," Joe said.

Jasmine shrugged. "Just take it one day at a time. Breathe. Nobody has their whole life figured out, written down in bullet points. We're all pretty much winging it."

"Even you? You seem like you've got things pretty much nailed down, Jasmine."

She laughed. "That's rich. I didn't even know if I was going to college for sure before I got the acceptance letter from Wildwood. I was half tempted to use the money I saved up just to travel."

"But now you're here," Joe said. He finally sat back, rubbing his eyes as he sunk into the chair. "And so am I."

"You'll get there," she said. "But not without some help. You might want to start thinking about reaching out. There are organizations-"

His eyes snapped open. "If I tell them about my life, I'll just get into trouble. I don't know how, but it'll all come back to that rest area. You know they don't like charging cops with murder. Somehow they'll pin it on me and..."

He seemed to shiver from head to toe, as though the cold of that winter blizzard was still sunken deep in his bones.

"I get why you're paranoid," Jasmine said. "But take it from me, a gal who has her head on reasonably straight... who has something of an understanding of how reality works. No one's going to blame you for what happened to Kirk. We were all there, we can all testify about what really happened. And no one's going to care that you spent all those years in the rest area. When you talk to people about that kind of stuff, there's a thing called confidentiality that comes in."

Joe nodded slowly, let out his breath. "I'm sure you're right."

"I usually am," Jasmine said, beaming. She checked the time on her phone, then jumped to her feet. "Crap, I gotta go! Hey, since you're going to be taking over my living room tonight, I'm bequeathing you the honor of giving Luffy his dinner. Kibble's in the closet. If he's really good, he can have a little bit of whatever you eat."

"Just a little?" Luffy asked, his eyes as big as saucers.

"I don't have any food," Joe said.

"Yeah, but I do," Jasmine called as she disappeared into the bedroom. "There's some random leftovers in the fridge. Some junk in the freezer. If you get really creative, there is some actual fresh food in there too. You could whip up an actual dish of some kind."

She shut the door so that it was only open a crack. Of course, Luffy nosed it halfway open and came in to watch her change. The fact that he could speak English, at least inside her head, made it all feel a bit strange. But she just had to remind herself that he was, in fact, a dog, and not a person stuck inside a dog's body. At least as far as she knew.

Getting ready for work was as simple as slipping her shirts and pants off and slipping new ones on. A dark, collared short sleeve and a pair of gray jeans she'd brought from home. She slapped the visor on her head, fixed her hair into a ponytail, and grabbed her nametag as she exited the bedroom.

"I'm not going to bother taking my keys," she said. "Don't lock me out."

Joe nodded, looking glum as she shut the front door behind her. But not quite so glum as Luffy, who took her leaving for each shift like she was going off to war, and wouldn't be home for untold years.

"See you soon, buddy," she said under her breath as she hurried down the stairs.

Chapter 5

As Jasmine entered the next week of classes, she felt sick with worries and distraught with tension. Every shouting voice and every sudden noise made her heart pump with venomous fear. When she saw a student napping out on the grass one day, she assumed he had been murdered and was ten feet away, creeping up with trembling hands, when he suddenly rolled over and started looking at his phone.

Time wore on. The first vision seemed destined never to be followed up by a second. Days passed in perfect normalcy, and it was beginning to seem like the whole thing had been a fluke. A random vision connected to nothing, that meant nothing. Just to be sure she wasn't missing anything, she scoured the parking areas at Wildwood and asked around to see if something was going on. The only thing she heard was that the student council was vying for assigned parking. But that was just one part of a packaged proposal which included other things, such as renovations to the already well-appointed school. She assumed it meant nothing... and no second vision came to tell her otherwise.

By Thursday she was calm again, back to her usual self, no longer looking over her shoulder at shadows that weren't there. She went to class and work, she read books and wrote reports. She wrote some of her own stories for her creative writing class as well, and received glowing reviews from Professor Sampson.

But reading was what took up most of her time. It was a heavy week for her international fiction class, and she was reading heavy books that had been translated to English and were loaded with footnotes. She read things from Russian, from Mandarin, from French, and even something from Swahili. She read until her eyes burned, used some eye drops, and read some more. She was glad for the long hours at The Book Nook; they had primed her brain for these marathons.

It also helped that the professor of her international fiction class was a very nice young woman who had not yet been beaten down by decades of teaching into a curmudgeon like Keller or a loose cannon like Hawke.

Professor Lucille Whitaker was only six years older than Jasmine. She seemed to have an angelic aura around her, a radiance that could be felt as well as seen. Perhaps that was because she was pregnant with her second child; Jasmine had read somewhere that hormones during pregnancy could give women a certain "glow." But she couldn't imagine Lucille as anything but beautiful.

She was also a rather more lenient professor than some at Wildwood. It was a school with a long history of stiff scholars and strict rules, a trend which she bucked with surprising ease. Paradoxically, the students in her class seemed to do better than those of most others. At Wildwood, that was really saying something.

"Okay, class," Professor Whitaker said during their Thursday session. "Seeing as I won't see any of you until Monday, I think we ought to get our weekend homework in order. I guess we've all been doing more than enough reading lately, haven't we?"

The class groaned in agreement and Whitaker groaned right along with them, rolling her eyes and flapping a hand in her face. Then she leaned on a table beside which was stacked with identical books.

"So I thought I'd give you something easier," she went on. "I have here enough copies for everyone to take home. This is The Enchanted Wanderer and Other Stories by Nikolai Leskov. I'd like you all to pick one story, as short or as long as you'd like, and write a review of it. That's all. An honest to God critical review, stating all opinions and feelings you had while reading. Seeing as reviews are a very subjective medium, I'll be giving everyone an automatic A on this assignment. You just need to turn something in, and it needs to be at least a thousand words. That will be all."

That pretty much summed up Lucille Whitaker's class. She understood what so few professors seemed to, that a mind at rest was often a mind more capable of serious thought. When you filled your day up with too much busy work, it was impossible to focus your thoughts on anything beyond the scope of your own life.

Jasmine always left international fiction feeling buoyant and carefree. And so it was that Thursday. It was the very last busy day of the week. She had a shift on Saturday, giving her the next forty-eight hours to decompress. Other than an errand she had to run on campus tomorrow morning, she had nothing planned.

"We can go to the park," Luffy suggested as they walked down the busy hall.

"Sure," said Jasmine.

"Maybe you'll meet someone," Luffy added, trying to sound perfectly natural and casual but failing miserably.

"This isn't the first time you've brought that up," Jasmine replied. "Why are you so adamant about me 'meeting someone'?"

Luffy gave her a look of pure, canine innocence. "You just seem lonely. I guess you're not used to living on your own yet."

"I'm not on my own. I have you."

"You know what I mean. Sometimes I hate to admit it, Jasmine, but I know the truth. I'm a dog, right? Just because I can, you know, beam my thoughts directly into your head or whatever, doesn't change the facts. I'm not a fellow human. We can't talk about the same things. We can't share all the same experiences."

Jasmine laughed, ignoring confused looks from other students. "What are you talking about? We share everything. We're always together."

"Except when you go to work," Luffy grumbled, staring forward.

"We've talked about this. We were lucky to get into Wildwood. But not every place is forgiving about pets. Not that you're my pet, but that's what everyone else sees."

Luffy said nothing. Jasmine had no idea what he was in a tizzy about, so she decided to ignore him. The good thing about him being a dog was that he forgave and forgot in the space of seconds. You couldn't keep him upset for very long.

"Joe and I talked that night when he stayed over," Luffy finally said.

"Is that what this is about?" Jasmine asked. "Wait... did you say you and Joe talked?"

"Not like that, don't worry," said Luffy. "He talked to me and I just sat there and stared at him, tilting my head from side to side. You know, dog stuff. Little did he knew I understood every word. I really am the perfect spy. People will say anything when it's just me and them."

"What did he say?" Jasmine asked. "Something about me?"

"Not specifically, but kind of. He said 'people like us spend our lives alone.' He said some more stuff, but that was pretty much the gist of it. He said he didn't think he'd ever be able to make a true friend, and you were the closest thing. But that you two had the same tendencies... you're loners. And that was why you would never be as close as you could be."

"He said all that?" Jasmine shrugged. "I don't know what he's talking about. I'm not a loner."

"That's what I tried to tell him," Luffy said. "But he just thought I needed to go outside again. Anyway, I saw how miserable Joe was that night. And I don't want you to ever get that way. You've got a leg up on him because you have me and not just a stack of old books to keep you company. I might be man's best friend, but I don't know if I should be man's only friend."

"That's a bunch of crap, Luffy. I already have Alicia. And Charles, I guess."

"They're school friends. As soon as you get home you go back in your shell, Jasmine. Don't lie. If you were ready to open up and have friends, seems like you'd maybe invite them over or something."

"Invite Charles to Lockwood Village? That would be the day."

"Don't make excuses."

"I'm not."

"Sure you are."

Jasmine sighed. "Shut up, Luffy."

"Alright then, I will."

"Good!" Jasmine said.

They walked in silence down the wide side hall. To the right were doors into class rooms, spaced out. To the left were high windows, impossibly high they seemed letting in the slanting light of late afternoon. Amber beams of sunlight stabbed down onto the polished stone floors at an oblique angle, swimming with dust motes. By now most of the crowd had dispersed and it was just Luffy and Jasmine, their footsteps clicking and echoing in the huge space.

But Jasmine wasn't in the mood to appreciate the splendid architecture, or the deep sense of history that seemed to ooze out of every little filled-in crack in the ancient floor. She stared at Luffy, her heart aching, ashamed of snapping at him. He would forgive her right away, but forgiving herself would take a little longer.

So much for a stress-free period.

Soon they turned the corner into the so-called nexus of the school, a crossroads where two side corridors intersected with the main hall that stretched down the length of the main structure. A few people were passing by, looking small and widely spaced in the cavernous hallway, their footsteps echoing to even greater heights and fading into distant knocking sounds. It was here that Jasmine felt a change in her mind, a shadow passing over her thoughts, a premonition arriving like a kiss of cold air.

She found the nearest bench, outside the professors' lounge. But she didn't sit. Not right away. Instead she stood facing away from it, ready to collapse into it if need be, and held herself almost upright with a hand on the arm of the bench.

"Jasmine, be careful," Luffy warned.

She nodded, taking a deep breath. That was all she had time for. Suddenly she was someplace else, seeing things that had not yet come to pass.

When she came to she was still somehow on her feet, though wobbling dangerously like a drunkard trying to get her sea legs. She did collapse then, falling onto the seat, but in a controlled sort of way.

"What was that about?" Luffy asked. "You could have gotten hurt."

"I had to try," Jasmine replied, wiping sweat off her forehead. "I can't keep letting this sideline me. One day, I'm going to have one of these visions at a very inopportune time. I'm not going to allow myself to be vulnerable."

"Fair enough. So, what did you see?"

She frowned, trying to hold the image. "It was Alicia. She was in the gym locker room, crying..."

"It could be something," Luffy said.

"Or it could be nothing," Jasmine replied.

However, the sound of Alicia's crying kept echoing in her mind. It was a sound of pure and total anguish.

Suddenly nervous, she took out her phone and dialed her friend.

"Hello?" Alicia asked, sounding perfectly calm.

"Hey!" said Jasmine. "Where are you right now?"

"Halfway home, girlfriend. Why?"

"Oh. I was just wondering..." She looked at Luffy, giving him a nod. "I was just wondering if you want to hang out tonight. If you don't have anything else planned."

"Let's see... I was going to sit around in my pajamas and watch TV. But I guess I can do that just as easily at your place."

"Or I could come over," Jasmine offered.

"No, that's okay. I know you don't have a car. Just text me your address. I can be over at... seven o'clock?"

"Sounds great," Jasmine said, smiling.

Unlike with Charles, she was not worried what Alicia would think of the place she lived in. So she texted the address over and headed out of the building.

Chapter 6

Seven o'clock came and went, but Jasmine didn't notice. She was too busy cutting up cheese and meat, getting a tray of snacks ready. It was 7:15 when there was finally a knock at the door.

"I'll get it!" Luffy called, running to the door. "Wait, no, I can't. Jasmine, help!"

"Hold your horses," she called, washing and drying her hands, then hurrying out to the living room to open the door.

Alicia was there, considerably dressed down when compared to her usual attire. The leather shoes, khakis and buttoned-down shirt had been replaced by run down sneakers, loose shorts, and a t-shirt that must have been at least ten years old.

The two girls shared a bubbly greeting. Alicia stepped inside and Jasmine shut the door.

"So, this is the place," Alicia said, looking around.

"Yeah," Jasmine replied, biting her lip.

"It's nice on the inside," Alicia replied. "I like what you've done with it."

Jasmine laughed. "You mean all the posters on the wall? They were cheap and they covered up the nail holes from all the previous tenants. Are you thirsty, or anything?"

Luffy watched proudly as Jasmine played hostess. They ate and drank and laughed, sharing gossip about school.

"I heard that Professor Hawke has a secret lover," Alicia said at one point, her eyes going wide.

"Him?" Jasmine asked. "Well, I guess I can see it. If you said Professor Keller, I never would have believed you. Who'd you hear it from?"

"Just around," said Alicia, shrugging. "Apparently he forgot to turn off his phone and his texts were still up. Someone saw something a little racy."

"Like what?" Jasmine asked.

"I dunno, just something kind of juicy or something."

Jasmine made a face. "Juicy?"

Alicia grabbed a pillow off the end of the couch and threw it at her. "Fine, then! You tell the next story!"

It went on like that for close to two hours. Eventually the talk began to circle around the concept of boys. By making an insinuation about her and Charles, Jasmine was able to get quite a rise out of Alicia. But other than that, the other woman seemed guarded and quiet about the subject. Like she was hiding something, keeping something close.

And it was around that time when she began to be distracted by something on her phone. It kept buzzing, and she would keep lifting it off the cushion and typing out something with incredible speed, using her thumbs more efficiently than some people used their entire hands on a keyboard. With each successive message she sent, Alicia seemed to get more agitated, until she seemed to be positively fuming.

"Are you OK?" Jasmine asked. The question she really wanted to ask was Who are you talking to? But that was just her inquisitive nature acting up.

"It's my sister," Alicia said with a groan. "She's such a..."

She left the next word unsaid, but Jasmine was pretty sure what it would have been.

Another message came in, buzzing Alicia's phone. This time when she read it she made a loud grunt of anger and tossed it down. Her eyes suddenly filled with tears and she tossed her head back, hiding her emotions.

"Alicia," Jasmine said.

"It's OK," the other woman said quietly.

"Is there something I can do?"

"No. Unless you can convince that witch to help me out!"

Jasmine shifted, suddenly uncomfortable. "What do you need help with?"

Alicia sighed, sitting forward and grabbing her phone. "Nothing. I guess I should probably go. You don't want me around when I'm like this."

"It's fine," Jasmine said. "We're friends."

But Alicia insisted on leaving. It seemed no amount of coaxing would make her stay, and so Jasmine sat back and watched Alicia gather her things.

"Thanks for everything," Alicia said, sniffling and wiping her eye. "Maybe we can do it again some time."

"Are you sure you have to go?" Jasmine asked as a last-ditch effort.

Alicia nodded. She quickly looked at her phone, either checking the time or seeing if there were any new messages. Then she was gone. The sounds of her footsteps came for a moment, echoing down the stairs, than the soft rumble of her car engine, the crunch of wheels on the dusty drive, and that was it.

"It was nice having her," Luffy said, glancing sadly at the door. "She smelled good."

"Creepy," Jasmine said.

"What? I'm a dog." He came to join her on the couch, curling up beside her leg. "I wonder what that was about, her leaving so suddenly?"

Jasmine shrugged. She had no idea. And she wasn't going to pry into it... unless she had to.

To Jasmine's mind, no more heinous device had ever been invented than the alarm clock. Perhaps the nuclear bomb was close, but at least that had fallen out of popular use. Alarm clocks, however, had continued their reign of terror in bedrooms across the world, rousing people from their perfect rest, with their wonderful dreams not yet completed.

When her own alarm went off at 4:45 a.m., Jasmine sat up fast with a chill traveling down her spine. For once she was glad for being woken; the shrill klaxon issuing from her phone had rescued her from a horrifying nightmare.

She had been alone in cold, nighttime waters somewhere off the coast near Blackwood Cove. Sometimes she could see the buildings she knew so well, twisted by the lens of the dream. She would glimpse them through parting waves of mist that quickly crashed back together again, stranded in the murk.

And she was not alone. Every now and then as she swam, she felt something cold and slimy against her ankles. At first she hoped it was only a bit of seaweed or kelp. But the further she swam, and the more she felt it, the more it seemed like limp, dead fingers trying to pull her down.

She swam and she swam, screaming for help. The more she tried to reach shore, the more it seemed to recede, so that she was always at the same distance. She would swim for what felt like an hour, and when the mists parted she would see the shore just as far as it had been before.

She screamed for Luffy, but for once he wasn't there for her. She screamed for her mom and dad and she even screamed for Sheriff Lustbader and Marlon Gale.

But no one came.

Finally she began to grow tired. Her bones froze in the cold water and her joints seized up like they were made of rusty metal. Her strength failed, and she sank under the water for the first time...

And Jack Torres was waiting for her, half his skin sloughed off, his bones showing through. He grinned, welcoming her into death.

And thankfully that was when she woke, the breath catching in her throat. Luffy was already up, standing by the bed and wagging his tail. She reached over to turn off her alarm and gave him a few pets as she lay back down.

But before her head could hit the pillow, Luffy was shoving his own head under the back of her neck.

"No you don't!" he said. "You told me to make sure you got out of bed when your alarm went off. No more sleeping!"

"I couldn't fall asleep now," she said, grimacing as she shoved his head out of the way with her elbow. "I just need to lie here for a minute."

"Another vision?" Luffy asked.

"Just a dream," she replied. Because if that had been a vision...

Of course, it wasn't. In a few moments reality began to bleed back in, along with the early morning grogginess. There was nothing to be afraid of. Not yet, anyway. It was just her and Luffy in a quiet apartment, basking in the wonders of air conditioning.

She forced herself to get up at 4:47. Shuffling into the bathroom, she swallowed down a glassful of cold water and then splashed a little on her face. After brushing her teeth, she was just about good to go.

All she had to do now was get her running clothes on. A pair of comfortable socks, some shorts, and a tank top would do it. She could have dressed warmer, but she wanted to soak in as much of the cool air as she could before it went away. The short heat wave had passed and now they were back in the territory of the upper fifties, with rain in the forecast for three of the next five days. She would start the run cold, but by the end she would be sweating.

"Ready to go?" she asked as she shoved a couple of water bottles into her pack.

"Just about," Luffy said, wagging his tail. "But I may need to take care of some business before we start running. You know, drop some weight."

"Please say no more," Jasmine replied with a smile, pulling open her junk drawer to grab a bag.

They set out at an easy pace, taking the wide gravel shoulder of the main road for the first quarter mile. There wasn't much of a breeze; the chilly air hung heavy around them, charged with moisture and ozone. It had rained the night before. The grass and the trees to either side of the road were laden with droplets that continued to filter down with the softest of noises.

Only one car passed them before they turned off onto the footpath that would bring them the rest of the way. Soon they seemed to be lost in the forest, running down a tunnel that had been bored out of it. A few birds were just starting their dawn chorus, though the sun was still behind the horizon. Jasmine breathed in the forest air, smiling, thrilled by it all. She never felt freer than she was out here traveling solely under her own strength. On her own two feet, she felt like anything was possible. That she could go anywhere and be there in no time at all.

Occasionally they spotted a wisp of mist crawling across the path. They always seemed to dissipate before Jasmine and Luffy could reach them. Though they did not cling quite so heavily to the ground as the sea fog of home, they were nevertheless a welcome reminder of Blackwood Cove.

Other than a few faint reflections on her nightmare, death was the farthest thing from Jasmine's mind. She was focused entirely on life, on possibilities... she began to plan out her whole future during that run, dreaming as bravely and boldly as she used to as a child. She was aware that most of these ideas wouldn't stick, but it made her giddy to come up with them. She imagined herself crushing every course ahead of her at Wildwood, of being top of every class. She imagined landing her first job in the publishing world before she even graduated, and moving up the ranks with preternatural speed. She was a true savant, a genius of the trade. With her eye for quality, she could sniff out the greatest new stories and the most lasting new voices. She would publish the first works of authors who would go on to win major literary prizes and change the world...

Before she knew it, her GPS watch was chiming the fifth mile. She looked down and saw the time in which she had completed it; 7:15. Her fastest time yet. No wonder she found herself completely out of breath, her legs burning. Luffy was looking at her like she had gone insane, panting like a maniac.

"Sorry," she said. "I'll slow it down a bit."

"Hey, don't be sorry," Luffy replied. "Run as fast as you want. I can keep up."

He went against his own words by crying uncle less than half a mile later. Jasmine slowed to a cool down speed, jogging lightly through the curves in the trail that immediately preceded her arrival at Wildwood College.

The sun was just starting to make itself known, pushing the blue of predawn out of the sky and replacing it in waves of violet and red and orange. She could just see the orb of the sun through the trees to the east, masked enough by the foliage that it did not sting her eyes. She stared at it, entranced, until she tripped over the concrete block at the head of a parking space.

Looking around, she saw only three cars parked here. One was the Dean's. She didn't recognize it by sight, but it was parked in the assigned spot. The other two cars she didn't recognize, but she figured they must belong to administrative workers. She didn't think anyone else would be here so early.

They walked up the dewy grass toward the flank of the building. Jasmine took off her shoes and socks and let her tired feet luxuriate in the soft ground.

"Why don't you just do that all the time?" Luffy asked, staring at her feet.

"Because someone thousands of years ago decided people needed shoes," she replied. "And now we're all cursed with soft feet."

Luffy gave her a contented look, as if to say makes sense to me.

Up ahead, parked just off the curb on the road leading up to the main building's circular drop-off point, she saw another vehicle. This was a white van emblazoned with the logo of a New Market cleaning company, an outfit called Symkowski and Sons. They must be just about finished with their nightly cleaning, she thought. Its presence at this hour went against the image that Wildwood had cultivated for itself. It was always clean, and simply that. Clean without having been cleaned, prim and proper out of sheer force of habit, not because they paid a bunch of hairy guys with mops who liked cheap beer and fast food to come in each night and wipe the place down. At least, that was the image Jasmine had in her head of the boys at Symkowski and Sons.

The clock tower began to chime in 6 a.m. just as Luffy and Jasmine were approaching the giant vestibule of the main building. Both of them looked up at the tower, watching the giant hands move.

"Does something look wrong up there to you?" Luffy asked.

Jasmine stopped, shading her eyes from the rising sun as she scanned the tower. "No. What are you looking at?"

"I dunno," said Luffy. "Just seems like there's something missing. Oh well."

As they started walking again, the front doors opened a little ways ahead of them. A short man with muscle-bound arms stepped out, carrying a broom and dustpan. He had the Symkowski and Sons logo on his shirt and, smiling, Jasmine realized he was quite hairy after all. The man gave her a greeting nod and turned left, walking around the side of the vestibule.

As Jasmine reached the door and grabbed the handle, she was stopped dead in her tracks by a sudden screaming.

She turned to look at Luffy. His hackles had raised, and she felt like hers had too. The hair on the back of her neck went up, and the hair on her arms, and all the rest of the fine hairs across her body.

The two of them ran around the vestibule, following in the footsteps of the cleaner. They found him standing twenty feet away, slowly backing away from someone who was lying there on the paving stones.

Jasmine stared. Deep down she knew this was going to come. As soon as the first vision hit her, she understood that this was her fate. For whatever reason, through whatever higher power or just through the random chaos of creation, she seemed destined to live around death forever.

"Now I know what was missing," Luffy grumbled, looking up at her. "The railing."

And he was right. At the very top of the clock tower, above the face of the clock itself, was a little look-out platform. It was segmented up by heavy duty posts. The spaces between the posts were spanned by wrought iron railings. One of those segments was indeed missing from the top... and Jasmine saw it a second later, lying on the ground not far from the body.

Chapter 7

It occurred to Jasmine that this was already the second dead body she had seen, not counting the open casket funeral she had gone to as a teenager. The first had not shocked her as she expected it would, which at first made her assume she was tougher than she previously thought.

But the second body was a different story altogether, because it was someone she knew. The sight made her turn away, her stomach constricting and her eyes dancing with black speckles as she nearly fainted. She fell to one knee on the ground, panting in an effort to get her lungs working again. She stayed like that for a long time, hearing the cries and shouting around her only faintly.

"Call the police!"

"Call an ambulance!"

"Did you see anything? Did he fall?"

That last question struck as being monumentally dumb. Of course he fell. Of course that was what had killed him. She knew that part. She had already figured that out during the brief glance she had taken at the body.

If not for the visions, she was content to let that stand as the chief explanation, indeed the only explanation, for how he had ended up there.

But as she squatted there and tried to sort out her thoughts, she wrestled with another fact she already knew. Oliver Bridges had not died of an accidental fall. The visions didn't mess around with accidents. He had been murdered. He had been pushed.

By who?

Jasmine finally looked up at the sound of crackling radios. Two officers had arrived and were corralling the crowd away from the body. One of them, a young man with a mustache and a nervous twinkle in his eye, bent over and laid a hand gently on her arm.

"Miss Moore?" he said. "You need to come with me now. Just a short ways away, OK?"

She nodded and went with him, her eyes wandering over his badge. Officer Barrett, New Market PD. She was glad he was here, though he looked almost as frightened as she felt. But even the fear was beginning to fade away. This was out of her hands. Other than those stubborn visions, she had nothing to do with any of this. She had already solved two murders in the past few months... she had no desire to make a career out of it.

"Just wait here for a few moments," Officer Barrett said. "We'll be right back with you."

Jasmine nodded, turning away and stroking Luffy's back as the police did whatever they were doing. Tracing the body, putting up a cordon, taking photos...

"I can't believe it," Luffy said. "I know we've been around enough of it lately, but death still doesn't make sense to me. You're living and breathing and having fun, and suddenly a second later... it's all over. Lights out. Goodnight forever. Just seems strange to me, I dunno. Maybe it's just because I'm a dog."

"It's not that," Jasmine said quietly. "Most humans have trouble wrapping their heads around the subject too."

"But not you, right?" Luffy asked.

"Sure," she said. "Not me."

It was a total lie, of course.

"But it's all fine, right?" Luffy said, flicking his tail against her. "We're going to find out who did it, and make sure it doesn't happen again."

Jasmine shook her head. "Not this time, bud. This is a real town with a real police force. They probably don't get a lot of murders here, but it's not like Blackwood Cove department. For one thing, they don't need me. For another, I'd just get in trouble if I tried to butt in."

"So you think they can figure it out?" Luffy asked. "Without your brain on the case? I don't know about that."

Under other circumstances, Jasmine would have laughed. "Let me remind you that I had plenty of help back in Blackwood Cove. And I have the visions. They're like pieces of evidence that no one else can see. Kind of gives me an advantage, don't you think?"

"Who cares?" asked Luffy.

Officer Barrett returned a few seconds later, crouching to give Luffy a few scratches and speaking in a low voice.

"If you don't mind," he said, "I'd like to bring you and your friend here back to the station for a few questions. Routine stuff."

"So you don't think it was an accident?" she asked.

Officer Barrett gave her a friendly smile. "I'm not going to discuss that just yet."

"Well, you wouldn't be questioning people otherwise."

"Miss Moore," he said, "we treat everything as if it could be a crime. That way, if it somehow turns out to be, we don't find ourselves too far behind the curve."

"You're right," said Luffy. "This does sound like a real police department."

Jasmine stood up and followed Officer Barrett toward his police cruiser. Another witness, the cleaner from Symkowski and Sons, was already in the front seat, so she and Luffy got in the back.

"Watch your head," Officer Barrett said, pushing down on the top of her head with one hand as she folded herself into the seat. Force of habit on his part, she assumed.

The drive back to the department took Jasmine through some parts of New Market she hadn't yet seen... but she was far too troubled by what had happened to get a good look at any of it. Death was a funny thing. It came in waves. Initial shock gave way to carefree disbelief, which eventually gave way to horror and regret. She was in that third phase now, replaying her conversation with Oliver and lunch over in her head. Had she missed anything? Had there been some sign that he was in trouble?

The patrol car pulled into a sunny parking lot in front of a small, neat brick building. It looked like it had been there for quite a while, and on the way in Jasmine glanced over a bronze placard that confirmed this. She knew New Market was an old place, but she could hardly believe this department building had been standing for close to two hundred years.

Especially when they went inside, and she saw how modern the place was. There were steel benches along one wall, polished until they shone so bright they stung your eyes. An air conditioning unit kicked out air so cold it felt like she had entered a walk-in freezer, which was a welcome respite. But it was no surprise that the man behind the front desk was wearing a heavy jacket over his normal uniform.

"Mr. Symkowski, you can wait here," Officer Barrett said. "I'll just take Miss Moore back for now. Another officer will be along to take your statement."

"How long's it gonna be?" the cleaner asked in a rough voice. "I gotta go before my wife leaves for work. Someone's gotta look after the kid."

"It won't be long, I promise." Officer Barrett turned toward Jasmine with a smile. "All ready?"

No, she was not ready. A half hour ago she had been enjoying the morning, as carefree as she could remember being, ready to start the weekend... and now she was immersed in yet another nightmare, this time in a big place she knew very little about. She felt like an alien, an outsider. Most of all, she felt frightened.

Barrett led her back into a small room. It was an interrogation room, quite obviously, but he did his best to make sure she was comfortable. She requested a cup of black coffee and a donut. Both were brought to her. Barrett sat alone on the other side of the table, patiently watching as she stirred sugar into her coffee. There was a digital recorder in the middle of the table, but Barrett had not yet hit record.

Jasmine glanced at the mirror on the wall.

"Are we being watched?" she asked.

"No, it's just us," Barrett said with a smile.

Jasmine thought it was an innate thing in most people to distrust the police. People from big cities, and even large towns like New Market. But she had grown up in Blackwood Cove, where there were only a few officers and you ran into them at the grocery all the time. You got to see them in their civilian clothes, and you got to look into their shopping carts to see what sort of thing they liked to eat.

They were just people, residents of the same town, friends and neighbors. And she got that sense from Barrett straightaway. He gave off that sort of Norman Rockwell vibe; young, a bit plump, rosy red cheeks and an easy smile. There was no doubt in her mind that he was telling the truth. She had the feeling that his mother had taught him better than to lie.

By now her thoughts were starting to clear. All she felt was fear, rather than confusion. Fear and sadness. Her mind was clicking along, working as efficiently as it usually did. She understood things now that she had missed a little while ago.

"How do you know my name?" she asked.

"Hm?" Barrett looked up at her from checking his fingernails.

"You've referred to me as Miss Moore several times," Jasmine said. "How did you know my name? Unless I gave it to you while I was in shock and don't remember."

"That could have happened," said Barrett. "People say all sorts of things when they're in shock. I once had a woman admit to me that she was having an affair. Unfortunately she was my girlfriend."

He paused, grinning across the table.

"No?" he said after a moment, when it was plain Jasmine wasn't going to laugh. "Well, don't pity me either. I stole that joke from a comedian I was watching the other night. The truth is, I knew your name before I showed up at Wildwood this morning. I had heard you were attending, but I didn't expect to run into you. Forgive me for saying this, but it seems like death has an odd habit of happening around you."

"Yeah, I kind of noticed that," Jasmine said. "Let me guess... only it won't be a guess, just an obvious conclusion. You know me from the story Julie Barnes wrote."

He nodded. Then he stuck his hand across the table. "The name's Luke. Pleased to meet you."

"Jasmine," she replied, giving his hand a halfhearted shake.

"It's really cool to meet you," Luke Barrett went on. "I'm a big fan of yours, Jasmine. I think what you did in Blackwood Cove was really something special. It takes a brave person to rise up and spearhead any sort of movement like that, especially a murder investigation. Seeing as how often entire police departments bungle investigations like that, it really was something special."

A good portion of Jasmine's fear suddenly evaporated.

"We've got a fanboy," Luffy said from beneath the table. "You're on your own on this one, Jasmine."

"I'm glad you liked the story," she said. "But I'm not an investigator, a private detective, or any of that stuff. I'm just a student. A witness."

Barrett got the hint. He reached out and hit the record button. "Right. A witness. So I should ask you some questions. Right now we're obviously still establishing a time of death. We'll know pretty soon but, uh... did you hear or see anything strange when you arrived on campus this morning?"

"Just the cleaning guy screaming his head off," she said. "I was pretty surprised his voice could go that high."

Barrett snorted with laughter, shaking his head a couple of times to try and get back to business. "And what time did you arrive?"

"Just a couple minutes before I saw the body. Someone in one of my classes was going out of town and didn't have time to drop off their homework, so they asked me to do it. I had to get a book from the library, so I decided I could kill two birds with one stone."

"Alright," said Barrett. "The identity of the deceased has been confirmed. He was a student named-"

"Oliver Bridges," Jasmine said.

"You knew him?"

Jasmine shrugged. "Not really. I spoke with him once, not too long ago, at lunch. He was studying philosophy. He seemed nice. A little shy."

Officer Barrett looked troubled. "I knew his family. I'm surprised you don't. Does the name Lyle Bridges mean anything to you?"

She shook her head. "I haven't been in town for very long, and I've been kind of focused on my schoolwork. Sorry."

"Well, Lyle owns Pineapple," Barrett said.

Jasmine was waiting for him to say something else, to add another word or two onto an obviously incomplete phrase. But Barrett's lips were sealed; he was staring at her expectantly, like he thought the light bulb out to be turning on any second."

"Huh?" she said.

"Pineapple," he repeated with a chuckle. "You've never heard of Pineapple?"

"Can't say I have. Unless you're talking about the fruit."

"Don't be ridiculous Jasmine," Luffy added. "How could one man own a whole fruit?"

Colonialism, she wanted to say, but she didn't want Barrett thinking she was crazy. Although he sounded a bit crazy himself, spouting off the word pineapple all willy-nilly with no context.

"It's a restaurant," Barrett said. "A fine dining place here in town. The reason I'm surprised you haven't heard of it is because it's sort of like New Market's claim to fame. People come from all around to eat there. Celebrity chefs, and just plain celebrities. It's a pretty big deal. Won all kinds of awards."

"Oliver's dad owns it?" Jasmine asked. "I guess he must be a pretty big deal around here too."

Barrett grinned. "Getting curious, huh? I thought you were just a student."

She shrugged. "I can't help it. It's in my nature. You can just ignore my questions if you want."

He shook his head. "Wouldn't dream of it. You could say that Lyle is a big deal in New Market, yeah. Wildwood was the original reason why anyone outside the town ever heard of it, but Lyle's put us on the map globally. Pineapple is one of the most respected restaurants in the world, you know."

Jasmine found that hard to believe. She suspected this was all a bit of small-town hyperbole, an overly proud resident hyping things up. Then again, she wasn't much of a foodie. Her idea of fine dining was a cheeseburger and fries. It was safe to say she was ignorant in this specific arena.

Meanwhile, Barrett was back to looking miserable. Wringing his hands, shaking his head.

"You know why I signed up to be a cop, Jasmine?" he said. "It's because I love this town. I love everything about it, and I didn't want it to change. I see what's happening in the world out there, the world around us... There's violence, evil, corruption, all that bad stuff. And I just didn't want all that seeping into my hometown, you know? I wanted to keep it pristine. I wanted to know it was possible."

He shook his head, as though dispelling a juvenile thought. But Jasmine didn't think it was juvenile at all.

"I think that's the right reason, Officer Barrett," she said.

He shrugged. "Maybe. But it seems like I failed, right? Killings just don't happen here, no more than they do in Blackwood Cove. Sure, we have a lot more people, but none of them ever murder each other. We keep the peace. Not just the police, but the average citizen. It just isn't right that Oliver died."

He sighed, sitting back in his chair and rubbing his face. The digital recorder went on listening, copying every sound down in perfect fidelity. It did this job silently, but Jasmine still imagined the whirring, clicking sounds of an old-fashioned tape recorder.

She just sat still and let the situation play out. What had started as a witness interview had suddenly become a confessional of the unlikeliest kind. A small-town cop speaking his fears to the new kid in town. If this was a movie he would be driving her out of New Market, blaming her outsider ways for everything that had happened. Instead, he was spilling his guts... but she got the impression that if it wasn't to her, it would have been to someone else.

Jasmine said nothing. She just pretended she was a set of ears or, better yet, a mirror. It was better that Barrett bared his soul to her, because another person might not be so understanding.

"I thought I was brave," he said after a long moment. "What braver thing than to slap on a badge and a gun and swear to protect your community? Especially since I'm afraid of guns. But I guess I'm not brave, because the first thing I thought when I realized it was Oliver... the first thing I thought was that I hoped it wouldn't be me who had to tell his father."

Barrett seemed to be on the verge of tears, but he suddenly seemed to realize where he was and who he was with. He sniffed a few times, quickly wiped his eyes, and forced on a smile as he gazed across at Jasmine.

"Well," he said, "probably not what you were expecting when I brought you in here. Sorry about that."

"It's perfectly fine," she said. "You're allowed to have feelings too."

"I know. But I shouldn't have let them out like that at work. It's unprofessional."

Jasmine shrugged. "Good thing I'm not a professional, then."

Barrett laughed. "You're a good kid, Jasmine."

"You sure about that? For all you know, I might have been the one who killed Oliver."

"Yeah, sure. And I'm Queen Elizabeth."

Something else occurred to Jasmine just then.

"This whole time we've been talking," she said, "you've made it sound like Oliver's death was a murder. Am I missing something here?"

"Nothing that I know of," said Barrett. "But the way I see it, if anyone was gonna pull a dumb stunt and fall off the top of that clock tower, it would be one of those party kids. You know who I mean. They use their parents' money like a free pass through life, living it up while everyone else is studying."

Jasmine nodded. There weren't many people of that description at Wildwood, but there were certainly a few. Charles Dane almost qualified, except that he actually had a goal in life.

"It wouldn't have been Oliver," said Barrett. "He was one of the nicest, calmest kids you'd ever meet. Definitely not the kind of kid to go wild and kill themselves by accident. Almost always had his nose in a book and never bothered anyone. Not to say he was some kind of loner... He was shy, sure, but he had friends. Everyone liked him."

"If he was murdered," Jasmine said, "then there's at least one person who didn't."
Barrett frowned. "You're right about that."

Chapter 8

As she walked home from the police station, she missed out on yet another opportunity to explore the town. All she could focus on was her feet, the flow of traffic, the changing of lights at crosswalks. At one point a cyclist nearly crashed into her, and she barely heard his apology. Another person approached her with a stack of flyers, preaching something about the coming of the Antichrist. She just shook her head and kept walking.

"This place is crazy!" Luffy remarked. "Everyone here is a total loon! Jasmine, aren't you bothered by this?"

"By what?" she asked idly.

"This concrete jungle! What else?"

"Luffy, New Market has only twenty thousand people. Maybe someday I'll take you to New York or Tokyo. You'll really lose your mind then. Maybe I'll even have to scrape it up off the sidewalk for you."

"Funny," he grumbled. "Would you just look around? Look, there's another park! Looks lovely, doesn't it? There's a duck pond. Look, there's a little girl feeding the ducks! That's just precious. Right, Jasmine?"

She shrugged, glancing toward the park for a moment but taking in no details.

"What is it with you?" Luffy asked.

"What? I'm just walking."

"Don't play dumb with me, Jasmine. Maybe you can trick other people, but not me. I know you. You can't stop thinking about the case, can you?'

"There is no case, Luffy. Not as far as I'm concerned."

"There you go, lying again. You really need to make up your mind. I don't care what you decide to do. I'm your friend; I'll stick with you no matter what. But all this back and forth and flipping and flopping... it can't be good for you. One second you're adamant that you never want to be a part of another investigation. Now Oliver's death is all you can think about."

She looked down at him, smiling sheepishly. He really did know her too well.

"Care to share with the class?" he asked, borrowing a phrase he had heard Professor Hawke use on numerous occasions.

"Okay it's like this," Jasmine said. "Barrett seems pretty much convinced that Oliver's death involved foul play. Is it intuition, or is there something else going on?"

"You mean, you think Barrett could have killed Oliver?" Luffy asked. "That guy? He probably still sleeps with a teddy bear and calls his mom every night."

"Watch what you're saying," said Jasmine.

"You call your mom every other night. There's a difference. But back to my point..."

"No, I don't think Barrett has it in him. But who knows? And even if he had nothing directly to do with Oliver's death, he might know something we don't. Something that happened in the past, some enemy who might wish harm on the Bridges family. We're really in the weeds here, Luffy. In Blackwood Cove, we knew everyone. Even if we didn't always know what was going on, we knew how to find out. It was different. Simpler. Now we're in New Market. There's a whole other set of dynamics here."

"Jasmine, sometimes you need to just think like a dog," Luffy said.

"What does that mean?"

"It means, think small. You think I stare at the stars all night and think about whatever humans think about? You think I wonder if there's other life out there, or what it would be like to colonize another planet? No. I just think about how pretty the stars look and move on."

"What's your point?" Jasmine asked.

"My point is, you're thinking too big. It'll hurt your brain. Humans are smart, right, but you're only just smart enough to get yourselves hurt. Start thinking smaller. Maybe it's not about New Market and all twenty-thousand or whatever people live here. Maybe it's just about Wildwood."

She nodded slowly. He might have a point there.

"And anyway," Luffy went on, "let's go back to what you said about this not being Blackwood Cove. We aren't dealing with Sheriff Lustbader and his small band of well-meaning knuckleheads. There's nothing you can do here, unless the cops miraculously decide they're in over their heads and ask for your help. You get me?"

"I got you."

"So stop worrying your head over it."

"Okay," she said, taking a big breath. "I'll try."

"First order of business, enjoy the moment you're in. Get out of your thoughts and look around."

She did so, and suddenly realized she was right in front of a beautiful florist's shop. The perfume of a dozen different flowers wafted out at her. A little ways up the street, a mailman was performing his rounds on foot, hoisting a huge sack, waving and smiling at the people he passed. Behind, a young woman and her two-year-old daughter sat on a bench, enjoying ice cream from the parlor behind them.

There was a man with them, bending down to tie his shoe... and when he sat up, Jasmine recognized him suddenly.

It was the man she so often saw walking around Wildwood in the evening. The unknown stranger who was neither student nor staff.

And the woman beside him, Jasmine realized, was none other than Lucille Whitaker, her international fiction professor. She had been hard to recognize at first, under the huge sunglasses she was wearing. But as she turned to wipe her daughter's face, the large bump formed by baby number two was obvious.

Feeling a sudden and inexplicable stab of fear, Jasmine turned on her heel and hurried mechanically up the street.

"Park?" she asked.

Luffy was far too excited by that single word to notice the change in her demeanor. Jasmine walked up the next crosswalk, crossed the street, and doubled back to reach the same park they had passed earlier. She hid herself away in the shadows of the trees, letting Luffy run around and chase bugs while she tried to calm herself down. The dog was right; she was thinking way too much.

Chapter 9

The weekend passed in a slow, confused blur. Rather than enjoy her relaxation period, Jasmine felt like she was rotting away in inactivity. She had the feeling that she should be doing something useful... but no amount of reading, writing or studying would get rid of the feeling. Going to work didn't help either, though it distracted her for a few hours.

Finally, the dreaded day arrived. Monday. She had heard through the grapevine, or rather through a terse text from Charles through a conversation they normally only used to organize their rides home, that Dean DuPont would be giving an address to the entire school at noon. That was well enough, because it got her out of her least favorite class, but for some reason she dreaded seeing any of her fellow students.

It took her until mile three of her jog to figure out what was causing the dread.

It was guilt.

She didn't understand that either for a little while. But after reflecting on what she and Luffy had talked about on Friday, she realized that the guilt came from the same place as the dreadful feeling of wasting her time. Deep down, some stubborn part of her assumed that she ought to be out there investigating. That, since she had taken part in two successful cases, she somehow owed it to New Market and Wildwood College to solve the thing.

It was a silly notion. But as with so many other silly notions, the knowledge that it was silly did nothing to dispel it.

For no purpose other than to vent her frustrations, Jasmine picked up her pace and blazed onto campus at a dead sprint. Students on the path took one look at her and quickly shuffled out of the way. Luffy tore ahead of her, absorbing her energy, barking and wagging his tail at everyone he passed.

They finished their sprint outside the gym. Jasmine bent over with her hands on her knees to catch her breath, staring at the ground as little drops of sweat fell off the tip of her nose and darkened the paving stones. Darkened them like blood...

Shaking her head, Jasmine stood up abruptly and hurried inside the building. The huge wrestling mat was empty. No sparring happening this early, and apparently no pilates classes. Perhaps the instructor had used the death of Oliver Bridges as a convenient excuse to take the day off.

In a moment they were stepping into the female locker room. Luffy heard it first, his ears perking up, letting out a sympathetic groan. Jasmine heard it a second later; the sound of someone sobbing, muffled and distant.

She frowned in sympathy but went on her way, visiting her usual bench to start pulling out a fresh change of clothes. It wasn't the first time she'd heard someone who thought they were alone, crying out their woes in the locker room. A boy broke their heart, a professor used harsh language in critique of their work.

But then she remembered her vision.

"Crap," she said, cramming her clothes back in her bag and carrying it across the room.

As she came closer to the toilet stalls at the back, she recognized the sound. She had heard it twice now. Once in her vision, once at her apartment. And now Alicia was crying again, pitifully and brokenly. She made sounds that could not have been caused by a breakup or a bad grade. This was real, deep hurt, the kind that might not ever heal.

For a long moment Jasmine wrestled with the question of whether to leave her friend alone or offer a shoulder to cry on. Finally, during a lull in the sobbing, she shuffled around a bit to make it clear she was there and then knocked on the stall door.

"Alicia?" she said.

"Go away!" the girl shrieked.

Jasmine and Luffy both jumped in surprise, then turned to walk away. They hadn't made it four steps before the stall door banged open behind them.

"Jasmine?" Alicia said.

Jasmine looked back, trying to smile. "Hey, kid."

"Sorry," Alicia replied, wiping her red, puffy eyes with a tissue. "I didn't know it was you at first."

"It's OK, I shouldn't have interrupted."

"No, it's fine. I just figured you were one of those witches on the track and field team who live to torment me."

Jasmine crossed the space between them and wrapped Alicia in a tight hug.

"Is it anything you want to talk about?" she asked.

"Not really," Alicia said, her voice shuddering and heavy with misery.

Jasmine held the girl at arm's length. "Well, I'm here if you change your mind. I mean it."

Alicia nodded. "I know. Don't you have to get to class?"

"And so do you," Jasmine said with a smile. "I just need to shower really quick, then we can walk over together. How does that sound?"

Alicia smiled too, wiping another tear from her sunburned cheek. "Okay. Luffy will keep me safe, won't you boy?"

"Absolutely!" Luffy barked. "Safe from what, I don't know. But if whatever it tries to mess with my friends, I'll do a number on them that'll put a chainsaw to shame!"

Jasmine's eyes went wide and she nearly lost her balance. She shot Luffy a warning glance, but he just looked up at her innocently. It was a game he liked to play sometimes. Say something shocking, try to get a reaction out of her in front of other people. He thought it was a riot, but Jasmine hated it.

No one in the world knew what she and Luffy shared, or about her visions. So far, she had no intentions of changing that.

The morning session with Professor Hawke was a heavy one. Unnecessarily so, Jasmine thought. He veered away from what they had been discussing lately and touched on a number of books, essays and short stories that dealt with death. Perhaps this was some attempt to get them ready for the heavy emotions that were sure to be flying around at DuPont's talk, but Jasmine thought it was more like Hawke hadn't come up with a good lecture for today and decided to go for the easiest option. He did not strike her as a warm man, and as far as she knew Oliver Bridges wasn't in any of his classes. But perhaps this was an unfair assessment. After all, she didn't know the man all that well.

"Where's Alicia?" Charles asked quietly, ten minutes into the lecture.

Jasmine glanced to her right and saw an empty seat.

"I didn't even see her leave," she said.

"I did, but I figured she had to visit the restroom," Charles replied. "I advise that you keep a close watch on that girl, Jasmine. She hasn't been right since the news went out on Friday morning. Come to think of it, she wasn't right directly before that either."

"How do you know?"

"Because I was with her," said Charles.

"With her? On Friday morning?"

He nodded, staring vacantly toward the front of the class and doodling random shapes on paper to make it look like he was taking notes. "You know Alicia. Always waiting until the last second to finish things. She asked for some help with an assignment she had due that afternoon."

"And you just decided to do it out of the kindness of your heart, right?"

Charles shook his head. "Heavens, no. I did it in exchange for a favor."

Jasmine rolled her eyes. "Please. What on Earth could Alicia Newman have that you don't?"

"A face you don't want to punch," Luffy said.

"Fair enough," Jasmine replied.

"What was that?" Charles asked.

"Huh? Nothing."

"Well, to answer your question, she has connections of the feminine variety."

"Wow, did you really just say that?" Jasmine asked.

"I did. And if you would let me finish, perhaps you wouldn't think it was such a foolish thing to say. Or perhaps you would. That's your prerogative as a sentient entity."

"Big words," Jasmine said.

Charles shrugged. "We are sitting at Wildwood College, a place known for its English language programs."

"Touché. Sorry for interrupting... what were you saying?"

Charles grunted in frustration. "I was saying, essentially, that Alicia is good friends with a girl I happen to fancy."

"Ooh, who is it?" Jasmine asked.

"That's not your concern. I was just trying to explain why I was with Alicia so early on."

At that moment, a piece of chalk came sailing up the rows of seating and hit Charles square in the chest. He jumped in his seat with such energy that he knocked his fake notes to the floor.

"Quite a conversation you two seem to be having," Professor Hawke called out. "Care to share with the class?"

"No, sir," Charles replied. "In fact it was rather boring. We were simply discussing what effects the writings of Thomas Paine might have had on the French Revolution. Your earlier mention of the guillotine put us on a bit of a tangent, I'm afraid."

"As I was saying before we were rudely interrupted," Charles continued as they walked to their next class, "Alicia was acting out of sorts that morning, even before the news got round to us."

"Out of sorts how?" Jasmine asked.

"Just being quieter than normal. Preoccupied is a good word to describe it. She had more than enough time to finish that assignment, but it seemed she couldn't be bothered. Something more important was weighing on her, I suppose."

Jasmine told Charles about that night she had Alicia over to her apartment. The way she left in tears, the things she had said.

"I suppose that might explain it," Charles said. "She had some sort of family drama distracting her. When we heard about Oliver, though, she went very quiet. I left quickly thereafter, feeling quite uncomfortable."

"We should look for her," Jasmine said.

"I can do that," said Luffy. "I might be able to pick up her scent, you know?"

"You two have an absolute ball with that," said Charles, "but I have a class to get to. She and Oliver barely knew each other. I'm sure she'll get over it."

Despite their best efforts, asking and sniffing around the school, they did not have any success finding Alicia. Time was short, and Jasmine rushed to her next class, arriving just in the nick of time.

Professor Keller was as dry as usual. But this time he was dry in a depressing way. The empty seat previously occupied by Oliver Bridges stood out like a sore thumb, and Jasmine couldn't stop staring at it. Nothing of any great importance was discussed during the class, at least not that Jasmine could remember.

It was almost eleven by the time she left LnL. Not enough time before DuPont's talk to do anything useful, but too much time just to sit around. She and Luffy wandered through Wildwood, walking up and down each hall. When they exhausted interior options they took to the grounds, skirting the fields in a long loop, coming within a few feet of that unruly barrier that separated the remote college from the dense wilderness beyond.

Just when the fresh air was starting to help Jasmine get her head on straight, an alarm went off on her phone that she had set a little while ago. It was time to head back inside and find her seat in Wildwood's auditorium.

The last time she had entered that vast chamber was to get writing advice from a master of the craft, a published author who had been working in the field for twice as long as she had been alive. The energy in the hall today was decidedly different, quiet and somber. No one was ready with their phones to get video and screenshots. No one was carrying a book to be signed afterward.

Jasmine found Charles and took the nearest empty seat to him. She looked around, but didn't see Alicia anywhere.

The screech of microphone feedback pulled her attention to the stage.

Elden DuPont, the Dean of Wildwood College, was standing at the podium. He was a large man in every way it was possible to be large. Tall, broad, outspoken and egotistical. His family had been among the first to settle in the area, before New Market was even New Market, back in the late 1700's. This was a badge of honor that DuPont wore every day of his life.

Today, the large man seemed to be sweating a lot more than usual. He was dressed in a heavy tweed suit, but he was always dressed in a tweed suit. The sweat must have been caused by something else, Jasmine thought, but she couldn't imagine it was from nerves. She didn't think Elden DuPont had been nervous a day in his life. Why would he be? As far as she knew, the man had never faced a meaningful challenge. His position at Wildwood had pretty much been his birthright; everything had been handed to him on the proverbial silver platter.

"Greetings, brothers and sisters, sons and daughters of Wildwood," DuPont began. The only thing small and delicate about him was his voice, but it rang clearly through the silent hall. "We're gathered here today to pay respects to a fallen member of our family..."

Behind him, a giant poster of Oliver's student ID photo had been pasted to a moveable wall.

"Anyone who knew anything around here understood the truth of Oliver Bridges," DuPont continued, mopping sweat off his brow with a handkerchief. He was stuttering his words now, barely getting them out. "I had the pleasure of meeting with this bright young man on several occasions. There are those who might say Oliver's future success was already guaranteed by the fame and riches of his renowned father, Chef Lyle Bridges.

But I say to that, nonsense. Oliver could have been born in the lowest of places, among the most downtrodden of society, and he still would have found his way to greatness. He had a keen mind, an intellect so sharp you could cut yourself on it, if he hadn't been so nice. And that was the main thing about Oliver. He had a heart of true compassion, a rare thing in this world and something to behold. No grudge would ever have found a place in his heart, no hatred or anger. Only love and understanding. If he had been allowed to live a full life, I..."

For a moment it seemed DuPont had finally gathered steam. His tongue had started flapping, as though it were a windup toy and someone had finally found the key, and didn't seem liable to stop anytime soon. But suddenly he ground to a halt, the words falling out of his mouth and fading away. He abruptly bowed his head, falling forward against the podium.

"Sorry, I..." He looked up at the crowd, smiling or grimacing; Jasmine couldn't tell which. "I didn't think I would ever have to make a speech like this. I suppose I don't have the same kind of heart that he... that Oliver had, so perhaps I should just get to the practical details."

He cleared his throat, flipping through a few pages in front of him.

"First of all, the date that Oliver died will officially be marked as a special one in Wildwood's calendar, from here on out. On that day each year staff and students will be able to attend a special vigil in his honor, where various community outreach programs will be staged. A grand idea, but not mine... It's all thanks to Oliver's father, who unfortunately couldn't be with us here today. He and the entire staff of his restaurant Pineapple will help fund these programs in Oliver's name.

"Second, I want to say that we here at Wildwood are going to do our best to help the community of New Market heal from this awful tragedy..."

Chapter 10

Jasmine woke to two sounds.

First was the sound of rain. The heavens, having been clouded over with blankets of gray for the past couple of days, had finally decided to open. The rain was coming down in sheets, or more accurately in buckets. Glancing out the window, Jasmine was unable to see more than ten feet. Her visions was obscured not by mist or fog but by the sheer density of the downpour. It hissed and pounded at the pavement below, drumming on the cars, putting up such a din that she almost didn't notice the second noise.

She picked up her ringing phone as she hurried across the living room, wiping drool from the corner of her mouth. There was one window in particular in her apartment that always let the rain in, and she was suddenly soaked from head to toe as she rushed up and slammed it shut.

Luffy, curled up in a ball on the floor, blinked his sleepy eyes and glanced at her.

Jasmine checked the time as she brought the phone to her ear. It was a quarter past five. She had been home for almost two hours, and had spent most of that time asleep.

"Hello?" she said into the phone.

"Hello there, Jasmine," the cheery voice of Officer Luke Barrett replied. "Say, I didn't wake you, did I?"

"You might have. But I wasn't intending on sleeping that long anyway."

"Well, you're welcome. Anyway, you're probably wondering why I'm calling you back..."

"Not really. I just figured you maybe had a few more questions to ask me."

"Oh! Well, that would be a good reason," he said with a chuckle. "But actually... well, maybe it would be easier to explain if you just came on down to the station. If it isn't too much trouble, that is."

Jasmine glanced out at the rain, frowning. "It wouldn't be, except I don't have a car."

"Right! Well then, how about I just come by and collect you? Luffy can come too."

And so Jasmine and Luffy found themselves standing out on the covered second floor landing of their apartment building a few minutes later, staring out at the parking lot as it began to flood. The gutters were working overtime, ejecting torrents of water. The sidewalks were running over, the sewer drains were inundated. The lower sections of the parking area were starting to fill in, turning to temporary ponds where cigarette butts and dead leaves congregated and swirled around. Day had suddenly turned to twilight, the sun all but smothered by the heavy cloud cover. Everything existed under a gloomy grayness.

Before too long, the headlights of a police cruiser cut through the foggy wall of rain. Despite the place's reputation, it wasn't common to see a cop car at Lockwood Village. But a few people who had been loitering outside their doors, watching the storm, suddenly decided to retreat inside and lock themselves away.

The cruiser stopped just outside Jasmine's building, stabbing its cones of light out across the drowned parking lot. The windshield wipers swished back and forth at manic speed; the engine growled, its sound somehow amplified in the cold, wet air.

"Got your umbrella?" Luffy asked. "We're about to get wet."

In truth, Jasmine didn't own an umbrella. It was one of those little things that was easy to forget when you moved to a new place, like a ladle or a toothbrush holder. So the two of them were forced to run across the parking lot, splashing through puddles. The water was cool and sharp with the scent of ozone. The grass seemed to glow a brighter shade of green around them, as though picking up the charged quality of the air and emitting it.

It was actually rather fun, and Jasmine was laughing as she yanked open the door of the police cruiser and hopped into the back seat with Luffy.

Barrett cranked his head around to smile at her. "Would you believe the weather report has us down for a fifteen percent chance right now? Funny, huh?"

He faced forward and took the car out of park, driving slowly around the looping drive and heading out toward the road.

Jasmine's eyes were open this time as they headed for the station. But today there was little to see. A few lit-up storefronts, restaurants and bars where people gathered. Other than that, it was all gray, empty sidewalks and wind-lashed trees, releasing some of their fresh green leaves before a ripping torrent of wind. By the time they reached the station, though, the brief deluge had trailed off into a light sprinkle.

Instead of visiting that tiny interrogation room again, Barrett brought her to his very own desk. He had a decent sized cubicle in a fairly desirable location, less than ten steps from the coffee pot. But he seemed to lord over the space with the air of a humble diplomat. He had stuck up a few photos of a pretty young woman and an infant. His wife and kid, Jasmine presumed. Other than that, he hadn't put much of a personal touch on the place. He had also brought in a couple of chairs so that other people could visit him in his space. Jasmine sat in one now and Luffy, after giving Barrett a wary look, climbed into the other one. He curled up and began licking the rain out of his long fur.

"Like an oversized cat," Barrett observed with a smile.

Luffy stopped licking for a second. "And you look like a giant donut. What's your point?"

Of course, Barrett didn't hear. He had already turned to his computer and was clicking through a few windows, closing things out, opening other things. There seemed to be no rhyme or reason to what he was doing. It was just nervous fidgeting. Finally, he switched off the monitor and kicked at the floor, causing his chair to swivel around to face Jasmine.

"So, here's the rub," he said. "And this is gonna sound mighty strange... but I guess you're used to hearing strange things by now, maybe."

"I suppose so," Jasmine replied.

"What is this guy getting at?" Luffy asked.

"Picture this," Barrett said. "The other day... the day after Oliver was found, the chief of police here calls me into his office. Good guy, the chief. Name of Roger Sutton. You'd like him. Anyway, he sits me down, shares some fatherly advice. Stuff about how the world works, and how we all have an obligation to try and make things better. At first I have no idea what he's trying to say to me, but then he says, 'Luke, you've been working here for long enough. You've never disappointed me, and you've got all the makings of a great cop.' And then he gives me the case."

"We're calling it a case now?" Jasmine asked.

Barrett nodded. "Roger agrees with me. It looks really fishy. Until we exhaust all possible sources of evidence and find nothing, we're treating it as a murder case."

"So, how far have you gotten?" Jasmine asked. She realized after the words already left her mouth that it was a presumptuous phrase. As Luffy had said, this wasn't Blackwood Cove.

But Barrett seemed to like it. The words made him smile.

"That's what I'm talking about," he said. "You go after the truth, no matter what. You don't care about fake crap like boundaries and rules, you only care about what's universally right."

"I wouldn't say that," Jasmine said with a nervous laugh.

"Yeah, you should see her at school," Luffy added. "She's never even been late to class once."

Barrett shrugged. "My point is... Well, Roger told me to dig deep. He told me to do everything I could to find the truth. And if the truth is that Oliver killed himself, or that he just fell off the tower on accident, then so be it. He gave me permission to use any means available to me. Look... I'm not a great detective. I've read more mystery novels than I could count, but I've never been able to correctly guess the killer. Not once. So what I'm saying is..."

"You want my help," said Jasmine.

He nodded. "Just to be clear, you can say no. I won't hold it against you." "Gee, how thoughtful of you," she said woefully. This was it, she knew; the chance that stubborn part of her mind had been waiting for. The chance to get involved. But it was one thing to pine for it, and another to actually experience it.

"You can do it," Barrett said. "I know you can."

"Don't be so sure. Blackwood Cove... well, I had a lot of help."

"You'll have a lot of help here, too."

"And at that rest area, well, I guess I didn't have much help at all. I figured that one out on my own, just about. But it was a matter of necessity. I knew I was stuck there with a killer, so I had to figure out who it was. But here... I dunno."

"You're feeling the pressure. That's perfectly natural, Jasmine. You've got a string of successes under your belt, and now they're adding all this weight to your shoulders. But that's a good sign."

She shook her head. "How could it possibly be good?"

"Whatever fear or anxiety you're feeling, it's a sign that you really do care. This is important to you. And that's how I know you aren't going to fail. Now look at me, look into my eyes, and tell me honestly if this is an opportunity you want to pass up." She stared at him and took a deep breath. The answer was clear; she just had to be brave enough to admit it to herself.

"I'll do it," she said.

Barrett's smile couldn't have been much wider without the top of his head falling off.

"Awesome!" he said. "Now, you understand, this is kind of off the books. Off the record, you know. We aren't going to be able to pay you or anything."

Jasmine felt giddy, and guilty because of it. But more giddy than guilty, in the end.

"I didn't get paid for what I did in Blackwood Cove," she said. "I never even thought about that. I just wanted to help out."

Her words were true, and she knew it. But she couldn't help feeling like a bit of a jerk, like she was patting herself on the back for how noble and selfless she was. She was really starting to rub herself the wrong way. This morning, she hadn't even been able to look at herself in the mirror. Somewhere inside her, she was sad about what had happened to Oliver. Deeply, painfully sad. But what she felt when she thought of him was shame. It seemed wrong to be so excited.

Barrett seemed unfazed, however. She supposed he was used to it. You didn't become a cop just because you wanted to make your community a safer place. Some part of you had to enjoy the work, and the work occasionally got dirty, even in a small town. Did he ever feel shame? Did he ever have that sense of being dirty, of being covered in filth, that Jasmine had been living with ever since Oliver had died?

"First things first, I need to apprise you of the current situation," he said.

Opening a drawer in his desk, he drew out a folder. The tab at the top read BRIDGES, OLIVER. It was the case file, and Jasmine saw that it was hopelessly thin. When Barrett opened it, a single sheet of paper fluttered out and landed on the floor. Barrett apologized and dove for it, crumpling the edges with his clumsy fingers.

"Here we have a list of names," said Barrett. "These are people whom we've tried to contact for interviews, but for one reason or another they were unable to comply. Keep in mind that they aren't suspects, just people who we'd like to talk to. Or I guess you could say they're people I'd like you to talk to. They might not respond to the police, but they might respond to a nice young woman with a cute puppy dog."

Jasmine looked over the list, and was surprised by some of the names. The first two made her eyes widen, and the third took her breath away completely.

1. Lyle Bridges

2. Sandra Bridges

3. Joe Sanderson (drifter?)

4. Alan Keller, Language and Linguistics professor

Jasmine looked up from the list with a litany of questions running through her mind. She had to slow her brain down and pick one out at a time; otherwise they would all try and flood out at once.

"I assume Sandra is Oliver's mom?" she asked.

Barrett nodded. "Neither of his parents have returned my calls. That's understandable, right? Their son just died. But if this is a murder investigation, it seems to me like time is of the essence. I'd really like to know what they know. If Oliver had an enemy to speak of, I think they would be the ones to know."

"What about Joe?" she asked, which was the question at the forefront of her mind.

Barrett shrugged. "He's a drifter who came into New Market not too long ago. I've had a few complaints called in about him. Nothing major. Some loitering, or sleeping where he shouldn't be sleeping."

"Why is he on the list?" Jasmine asked.

"Someone called in a tip yesterday. They claimed to work at Pineapple but didn't give a name. But they said I should check this Sanderson guy out."

"Did they say why?"

Barrett shook his head. "They just hung up when I tried asking. I've been trying to track him down. No luck so far. Hard to nail down a guy with no address, I guess. I'll find him eventually, but maybe you'll have better luck."

"Maybe," Jasmine said, hoping Barrett wouldn't hear how fast her heart was beating. Though it seemed like he couldn't possibly not hear, it was so loud in her ears.

"As far as this Keller guy goes," Barrett went on, reaching over to tap the appropriate spot on the page Jasmine was holding, "he's the only one of Oliver's professors who hasn't talked to me yet. I'm sure he doesn't know anything, but in these kinds of cases we have to turn over every rock to make sure we don't miss anything. Especially in this case."

"What do you mean?" Jasmine asked.

Barrett fidgeted in his chair, wincing. "I hope you don't think I'm some kind of amateur, Jasmine. After this long, I should have a nice, fat case file full of potential leads. But I challenge anyone to find a lead here. As far as anyone can tell me, Oliver Bridges was loved by everyone who knew him. He never got angry, and he never angered anyone else. The only thing I can see that might have got him killed was his sense of right and wrong. Did you know he was on the student council?"

"He just got the position recently," Jasmine said.

Barrett nodded. "And apparently he's been going crazy with it. Trying to fix a lot of small issues at Wildwood that have been overlooked for years in favor of larger concerns. At least that's what I heard from talking to a few other professors. Could be he stepped on the wrong set of toes at some point, but hey; he was elected, so obviously the student body wanted someone like him to take charge."

"I know someone whose toes he might have stepped on," Luffy put it.

Jasmine nodded. She was thinking the same thing. She was thinking of a name that was not on Barrett's list.

"So you want me to talk to these people?" she asked.

"If you can. Whatever you find out, you can relay to me. I'll be conducting my own investigation, and no one will know we're working together. Sound good?"

Jasmine nodded. It wasn't too dissimilar to the arrangement she and Lustbader had been in Blackwood Cove. Except back then, she had a signed note from the Sheriff, and his outspoken support. Here, she was pretty much on her own. The cops wouldn't mess with her, but they wouldn't help her either.

She took a deep breath, letting her eyes close for a moment.

"Can I get a copy of this sheet?" she asked.

"Take it," Barrett replied, waving a hand. "I can print out another one off my computer if I need to."

"Okay." She folded the sheet and stuck it in her pocket. "I just need one favor from you, if you think you can swing it."

Barrett sat back, relaxing in his chair. "Hit me with it."

She told him what she had in mind.

"I'll see what I can do," he replied. "Good luck, Jasmine."

That seemed to be her cue to leave. So she stood up, shook hands with Barrett and made her own way out.

Chapter 11

On Tuesday morning, Jasmine showed up at Wildwood at her own leisure. She hadn't bothered setting an alarm the night before and finally got out of bed at a quarter past eight. However, she didn't wait around. She packed a quick breakfast away in her backpack, which had been emptied of all school materials. Text books, writing supplies. Everything was gone other than a single small notebook and a pen, along with another item she didn't know whether she would need; a secret weapon. The bag felt oddly light as she lifted it onto her shoulders and tightened the straps.

She took the six-mile journey at a light jog, hardly ever breaking below a nine-minute mile. She and Luffy shared few words; both of them were content to soak in the surroundings, becoming lost in their own thoughts. But whereas Luffy was probably imagining what it would be like to chase the chipmunks and squirrels, Jasmine was trying to plot out the course of her investigation.

Try as she might, there seemed to be no obvious way to connect to the web. She didn't know where Joe was, and the guy didn't even have a cell phone for her to call. She felt weird about approaching Oliver's parents, and she thought they were probably at home anyway rather than at the restaurant, which would make things more awkward.

So she decided to start with the easiest targets, the people whose whereabouts were known to her, and who were used to her presence.

As she reached the edge of the college grounds and slowed to a walk, she pulled out her phone and sent Charles a text; Meet me at lunch. We need to talk.

By then the rain was starting to fall again, a cold sprinkling down the back of her sweaty neck. Jasmine stowed her phone and picked up the pace, entering the gym just in time to hear a sudden lashing of rain behind her as another springtime deluge began, hammering the metal roof of the building with the sound of a thousand snare drums. The sound was repeated a minute later as she turned on a shower full blast and stepped into it.

Today, she had come prepared. Before starting her run she had stopped in at the local discount store and picked up a cheap umbrella, which she deployed as she stepped out of the gym building. Luffy crowded next to her, trying to catch the rain that dripped from the edge of the umbrella between his jaws.

"You're a dork," Jasmine said.

"But you love me," he replied. "So, what's first on the agenda? Who are we talking to?"

"Barrett's list is nice," she said, "but I'm not going to just take his word for it that he talked to everyone else already. I need to hear what Dean DuPont has to say."

"He has a lot to say, and none of it's very interesting. I almost fell asleep during that talk he gave. A lot of people were crying, but I dunno... I got the feeling he was lying through his teeth the whole time. You really think he cared about Oliver?"

"No," she replied. "He just cares about Wildwood. And its reputation. Which is why he's going to answer every single one of my questions."

"Sheesh. Remind me again not to murder anyone when you're around. You'd sniff me out in about ten seconds."

"Please don't become a criminal, Luffy. You'd be terrible at it."

"Terrible?" he asked in a huff. "You should have seen that kid last time we were at the park. He dropped half his sandwich on the ground and it was gone in less than half a second, like a magic trick. By the time his mom even thought to look for it, we were fifty feet away."

"I never saw that," Jasmine said.

"Exactly. Master criminal, here. As far as you know, I might have killed ten guys by now and you'd never know it."

"Sure, Luffy. Sure."

He pranced along proudly for a moment, then gave her a guilty look.

"By the way, you never did eat that second egg roll off your plate last week," he said. "You looked so confused when it suddenly wasn't there. Like you thought you were going crazy, or something."

"That was you?" she asked.

"My bad. But are you really surprised? It had chicken in it, Jasmine. Chicken."

A TIMELY MURDER

He had timed his confession well. They were just entering the main building. There weren't many people in the hall, but there were enough that she didn't dare respond.

The clock tower wasn't the only tower at Wildwood. There was another one, shorter and less regal, situated at the back of the building. It had no real title, and was usually just called the North Tower due to its location. That was where the Dean's office was, and had been for all the many decades of the school's operation.

The first floor of the North Tower was home to a small fleet of secretaries. They were old women, but they were the type of old women who never seemed to get any older. They were eternal, typing away at their keyboards, doing whatever work it was that they did all day. Jasmine hadn't the faintest idea, but the stern looks on the women's faces made it seem like it was the most vital thing in the world, the thread that was keeping this whole flimsy operation from crumbling around them.

"I just need to see the Dean," Jasmine said to the room, ignorant as to which woman in particular she needed to talk to.

"He should be free right now," one of them said, never taking her eyes off her computer screen, her fingers moving at lightning speed. "You can go on up."

Jasmine thanked the secretaries and approached the edge of the room, where a staircase led up onto the second level. The stairs were bolted to the wall, and followed its curvature, like those inside of a lighthouse.

The second level was home to a few offices. Some of the professors had separate workspaces here, but they were rarely used. The doors were locked. A heavy silence lay over everything, nearly as thick as the layer of dust that had been gathering for untold weeks. Jasmine continued to the third and final level, where an extravagant and huge waiting area played as antechamber to the inner sanctum of the Dean of Wildwood College.

She approached the polished mahogany door and knocked.

"Yes, who is it?" the familiar shrill voice called out.

"Dean DuPont, it's Jasmine Moore. A new student here."

All sounds from within the dean's office ceased, other than a prolong creak from his disk chair which soon faded into silence. Luffy's tail wagged nervously, tapping against the wall.

Finally, with another creak and a sound of two pieces of metal smashing into each other, DuPont came walking across his office to open the door. But he only opened it by a small amount at first, just enough for his large face to be framed within the gap.

"Yes, I know your name," he said. "Unfortunately, I'm a bit busy at the moment."

"No you aren't," she said. "Unless you're busy updating your own fan page in there."

He laughed at that, more out of shock than humor.

"Um, well, I suppose I could accommodate you in my schedule," he replied, his cheeks going red. He stepped back and pushed the door open. "Come on in."

She stepped through, nodding graciously at him.

"But not him," DuPont remarked, pointing at the dog. "I'm allergic."

"To dogs?" Jasmine asked.

"That's what I said. It was I who approved your request to bring little Luffy along, but that doesn't mean I want to snuggle up to him and inhale all that dander. I'm sure you understand that being able to breathe properly is important to me."

Jasmine stared at the man. He smiled, and she smiled back. She almost applauded him, and the way he had thrown her own snark back at her with good humor. Also, he had somehow remembered Luffy's name. Maybe he was better at his job than she thought.

"Did you hear that, Luffy?" she asked, glancing down at him.

He whined a bit, backing away into the hall. Jasmine shut the door slowly, making sure she wouldn't pinch his paw or tail.

"He won't get into any trouble out there, will he?" DuPont asked. "There's some expensive furniture in the waiting area that I'd rather not see covered in bite marks."

"He'll be fine," Jasmine said. "Luffy isn't like most other dogs."

DuPont nodded. "Yes, you made that clear in your letter, which is why I decided to let him become something of a student himself. Although I'm sure the only thing he's learned here is the rotation of lunch items. Would you like to sit down?"

They crossed the room to DuPont's desk, which was just as large and extravagant as Jasmine expected. It could have doubled as a table in a mead hall; its surface was mostly empty. As she sat on one side and DuPont sat on the other, the impression was of a vast gulf of emptiness between her and him, a gap bridged by an expanse of polished wood.

"So," DuPont said, folding his hands before him, "what can I help you with?"

"I have some questions involving Oliver Bridges," Jasmine said. She had learned a lesson from Blackwood Cove; sometimes it paid to hide your course of inquiry behind pleasantries, and sometimes it didn't. With DuPont, she felt like she'd get better results by being forward.

There was the faintest change in the Dean's body language. He shifted forward a little, going lower in his seat.

"I've already spoken to the police about that," he said. "I told them everything I know, which isn't much."

"Maybe you could reiterate what you told them," Jasmine suggested.

"To you, a student?" he asked. "I don't know about that."

She shrugged. "You said it wasn't much. What's the harm."

He licked his lips. "I guess there probably isn't any. Basically, I told them there's no way Oliver was murdered. The notion struck me as completely ridiculous. To most people, Oliver was invisible. He was quiet and he liked to read. To anyone who actually knew him, he was kind and soft spoken. Not the sort to make enemies."

"There's no one who could have wanted him dead," said Jasmine. "Is that pretty much the rub?"

DuPont nodded. "Pretty much."

Jasmine smiled. "Of course, some might say you have a bias here."

"Would they?" he asked, returning the smile.

"Yeah, they would. If this death is classified as a murder, it taints Wildwood. Instead of being known for its academic achievements, it'll forever be seen as the school where Oliver Bridges was killed."

DuPont sat back, relaxing a little bit now. "But you wouldn't say that I have that bias."

"I don't think so," Jasmine replied. "Because the alternative is worse. We have to think of what is implied if Oliver's death is ruled as an accident. He fell from your clock tower. He fell through a section of iron fencing that obviously wasn't anchored properly. It should have been pulled out and refitted, but it wasn't. So, instead of being known as the school where Oliver Bridges was murdered, Wildwood would be known as the school where Oliver Bridges was allowed to die due to negligence."

DuPont suddenly looked very uncomfortable. His relaxation had been short-lived.

"So," Jasmine went on, "you clearly have no reason not to fully cooperate with the police. Their investigation is the best chance of saving the school's reputation. But in the end, the truth will win out. Won't it?"

"That's the goal," said DuPont. "But you forgot the third possibility; that Oliver committed suicide."

"Did he seem like the type to you?" Jasmine asked.

"No, not at all. He seemed like a young man with a bright future who couldn't wait to get started on it. But mental illness is an insidious disease, Jasmine. It can infect anyone, even the most successful and seemingly happy among us. It doesn't discriminate."

"So, you think he might have killed himself. But not by simply jumping off the tower. No. He decided to throw himself straight through the weakened railing."

DuPont shrugged. "I hate to even imagine all this, it's quite nasty, but... consider this. He might have been climbing over the railing to jump, or vaulting over it, and it came loose as a result of his weight and force. Or perhaps... It is a sad fact, Jasmine, a very sad fact, that a lot of suicide victims who survive their attempts report a strong feeling of regret when they were passing the point of no return. It's possible that Oliver had such a feeling and reached out to grab the railing as he fell. His weight jerking suddenly on it may have been enough."

"Not if the railing was properly maintained," said Jasmine.

"Such a structural weakness may not have even been noticeable until it was too late," DuPont suggested.

"So, it's damage control time, isn't it?" Jasmine asked.

"For me, it's always damage control time," said DuPont. "I have a job to do, and I can't stop doing it just because something tragic has happened. As you said, the truth will come to light in the end. The police are working on it, and I am cooperating with them. There's nothing else I can do to aid the investigation. All I can do is to protect the school, insofar as it can or should be protected."

Jasmine nodded. "And I'm going to keep looking around. If that's fine with you."

"Actually, I'd prefer that you didn't," he said. "In fact, I would advise strongly against it."

"Well, that's nice. But I'm going to do it anyway."

DuPont grinned. "I can have you slowed down."

"You wouldn't dare."

"Why's that?"

"Because I know a man who's more powerful than the local police, and I have no problem calling him in if I need to."

She unzipped her bag now and pulled out her wrinkled copy of the Cove Herald. The front-page headline read LOCAL GIRL SOLVES MURDER. She slid the paper across the desk.

A TIMELY MURDER

"Take a glance at the photo there," she said. "Does that girl look familiar?"

DuPont frowned at the page. "Yes, I'm well aware of your exploits, Miss Moore. Don't think I accept any students here without knowing their backgrounds. I don't make decisions arbitrarily. Now, if you insist on taking this path instead of using your time at Wildwood as it was intended, I suppose I won't stop you. I just wish you would have more respect."

"I respect the truth," she said in response.

"Good. I'm glad to hear that. Now please leave. I have no more time for you right now."

He slid the paper back to her.

Jasmine stashed it away and headed for the exit, feeling a surge of confidence. This was going better than she had expected.

But when she was halfway toward the door, a familiar feeling washed over her. A rush of heat over her skin, followed by a burst of cold sweat and a sudden increase in respiration. She stepped faster, taking a slow, deep breath. Fighting it with everything she had, she gripped the door handle. Focusing harder than she ever had in her life, she forced her hand to move.

Please, she thought. Don't let me collapse in this man's office.

Maybe if she fought hard enough, she could block it out. Like ignoring a sneeze. The approaching vision would wash past her, never finding root, and it would disappear somewhere down the alleyways in her mind, never to be seen. Never to be known. Maybe she could take control, refuse these fits of premonition that kept assaulting her. But if she did, she knew it would mean throwing way invaluable evidence.

The door opened. She walked through it and pulled it shut behind her. Luffy was there, but she only saw for half a second before her eyes rolled back and her mind was swept along.

A tall blonde woman... bleached blonde, not her natural hair color... tan and well dressed, looking over her shoulder shiftily. Trying to hide, or watching out for someone. She approaches a small house where ivy clings to the brick, and she enters through the front door. Rain is falling... it is dark outside and getting darker...

Jasmine came back to herself, back to the waiting room at the top of the North Tower. Her legs shook violently, her knees knocking together, and she was aware of a strange choking, rattling noise coming from her own throat. She stopped it immediately, like waking up from a nap to hear yourself snoring for just a moment. Her hand was still gripping the door handle hard, and she was still standing.

"You did it again," Luffy said. "You managed not to fall over. How are you doing that?"

She released the door handle and stepped away fast as though it were a venomous snake. Crossing the waiting room, she lowered herself onto a seat as far from DuPont's door as she could get.

"I'm scared, Luffy," she replied, hugging him to her. "That's how I'm doing it. I'm just so scared of what might happen if..."

"Nothing will happen," he said. "You have me to look out for you. And if it comes to it, I won't let the bad people get away. I didn't in Blackwood Cove."

"I know," she said. "But I don't want to leave you alone. I want to learn how to fight this."

He licked her face a few times, then just sat there with his tongue hanging out, patiently waiting for her to be ready.

"There was a woman," she said. "She went into a house. I've never seen her or the house in my life, but I'll know if I see them."

"Good," said Luffy. "Maybe you should take a break for a while."

She shook her head. "I feel fine."

"You can call Brandon, or Sheriff Lustbader, or maybe our friend at the FBI."

"I'm not going to bother any of them," Jasmine said. "I don't need their help on this one."

"You mean, we don't," said Luffy.

"Of course. Always. We can do this, Luffy. The two of us. We'll beat those cops to the punch. How much you wanna bet? All the treats you'll ever get for the rest of your life?"

"Well..."

"Come on," said Jasmine. "You can be more confident than that."

"I can be, but I don't want to. Are you ready to go yet?"

Jasmine looked at the time. "We have some time to kill. How about we go for a little walk?"

Chapter 12

It felt strange, not being in class. But Jasmine felt no guilt for it. In her heart, she felt that what she was doing now was more important. More vital. At least for now. She kept telling herself that she could get back to work on her degree in earnest once this mess was wrapped up. But if she didn't do this, if she didn't try and figure this out, she would never have been able to focus on her work anyway.

Nerves had gotten the better of her earlier. Luffy had had his snack, but not her. When lunchtime came, she was ravenous. She quickly stuffed a biscuit into her mouth as she was walking away from the food line with her tray. And that was how Charles saw her, with her cheeks bulging out and bits of bread falling out from between her lips. He pursed his lips and turned away from her.

"Just try not to choke to death," he said as she sat down with him. "And if you insist on doing so, kindly move to another table."

"Come on, you wouldn't do the Heimlich on me?" she asked with a smile.

He stared at the bits of dough still stuck to her teeth. "If need be, I suppose I could give it a go. Please don't force my hand." His eyes moved to her tray. "You're not a very large person, Jasmine. How on Earth are you going to eat all that?"

"I have my ways," she replied.

"And she has me as a garbage disposal!" Luffy piped up.

Charles nodded as though it all made perfect sense and went back to his own food, cutting up a piece of plain chicken breast with a knife and fork and eating it very politely, dabbing a napkin against his mouth after each bite.

"Anyway," he said, taking a tiny sip of water. "I assume you didn't ask to meet so that we could discuss our dining habits."

"No," Jasmine said. "I won't try and hide my motives, Charles. You're too smart for that to work. I wanted to ask about Oliver."

The knife and fork stopped sawing at the dry bit of chicken. Charles set them down and reached for his napkin again.

"Why would you want to talk about him with me?" he asked.

"Because I'm talking to everyone who..."

"Who had a connection to him, yes?" Charles asked. "Who had a reason to murder him. That's what you're implying."

"I'm just looking at connections," she said. It was a half-lie, but she had always been good at those. Sometimes they were the only way to keep the peace.

"Then you're barking up the wrong tree," he replied, his hand shaking as he brought the water glass to his lips again. He took a much longer drink this time, and finally set the glass down.

"Weren't you angry at him?" Jasmine asked.

"Why should I tell you anything?" Charles shot back.

"Because I'm a friend and you want to help me."

"I want to help you, do I? Now that I know I'm a suspect in your little investigation? I'll tell you, Jasmine. I'll talk about Oliver Bridges this one time, but never again. He wasn't the lovely, innocent little sweetheart that everyone makes him out to be. He liked to read, yes, and that somehow means he was harmless. What a foolish sentiment. Oliver was a bulldog. He went after his position on the school council viciously. He wanted it, and he got it, but he didn't need it. Not like I did."

"Why did you need it so badly?" Jasmine asked.

Charles sighed. "What am I doing here? Digging my own grave. That's what I'm doing."

"Just tell me, Charles. If you didn't kill Oliver, you have nothing to worry about."

He nodded. "That's right. I have nothing to worry about. Nothing at all. Well, Jasmine, that council position was the last thing I needed. If I was able to display leadership capabilities, I would have received a summer internship at a publishing house I've wanted to work for since I was ten years old. Considering my connections, an internship would have guaranteed me placement there after graduation. Now, because of that Bridges git... I was this close." He demonstrated exactly how close by holding two fingers up. "He won over me by three votes."

"I'm sure you'll be fine," Jasmine said. "There's always next year, right? And Oliver is gone. I assume the council will be looking for a new president."

Charles shook his head. "No chance. They already defaulted to the vice president. You don't understand, Jasmine. I needed that position. Oliver didn't. He just wanted it so he could spread around those weird, idiotic philosophical ideas of his. He had his head in the clouds. He filled his mind up with the words of long dead philosophers, half of whom were probably insane, and that was the basis on which he formed his ideas of reality. He didn't know anything, and somehow he stole my dream from me."

Charles seemed quite calm as he went back to eating. He moved on from his chicken to a small pile of roast potato chunks, which he ate one at a time, chewing thoroughly.

"Do you know anything else about Oliver?" Jasmine asked. "Did you two have any prior relationship?"

Charles smiled at that. "I don't have much, Jasmine. But I know something you don't."

"What?"

"Not my story to tell. Ask Alicia, next time you see her. If she doesn't want to tell you, just pull that classic friend move and blame her for Oliver's death, like you did with me. I'm sure that will do the trick."

"I didn't mean it that way and you know it," Jasmine said. "All I'm trying to do is learn as much as I can. Why do you think I'm here, Charles? Meeting you in the lunch room? Because I think you're dangerous?"

"Some murderers aren't dangerous at all," he replied. "They kill once, under extreme circumstances, and then never again. Some of them even turn themselves in. I just want to ask you a favor, Jasmine. When the time comes, I want you to be the one who puts the shackles on me."

Jasmine shook her head. "Don't be a jerk."

"Why not? It's in my nature. Everyone seems to think so, anyway. Look, I've helped you out. I've told you why I was angry with the sod, and I pointed you to Alicia. Now I would like to eat in peace."

She nodded. "One last question."

"Let's hear it."

"Are you angry with me?"

He looked up, and saw the pain in her eyes.

"No, I'm not angry with you," he said. "I might as well be angry at a cat for hissing or a llama for spitting. Not that I would compare you to an animal. I only mean that seeking truth is in your nature, and tactfully conversing with your friends is not. I accept your faults, because it seems like you have already accepted mine."

Jasmine took her tray to an empty table and dined alone. But not quite alone. Luffy was always there, ready to pick up any scraps she might drop on purpose or by accident.

Jasmine had already left several voicemails on Alicia's phone. She had asked anyone who looked willing to listen if they had seen the young woman, but no one, including her scattering of other friends, could give her an answer. There was nothing to do but wait and hope.

She and Luffy spent the entire day at Wildwood. There was no use going home when there was still work left to do, but there was no work to do until later when the professors had time for her. So she visited them one by one earlier in the afternoon between classes, asking them if they didn't mind staying a bit longer this evening. They all complied, though with varying levels of stubbornness.

The halls of Wildwood were empty, echoing with the ghosts of footsteps, when she and Luffy approached her creative writing class. They stepped inside without knocking. A sea of empty seats filled the majority of the space, all turned to face the illuminated desk. Sampson Hawke stood by his chair, busily sorting papers and shoving them into his bag. His glasses were on the verge of falling off. He had his coat on and seemed completely ready to leave, but there was a mug of tea nearby, freshly steaming. Jasmine got the impression that she had only as long as it took him to finish that mug.

"Professor Hawke," she said. "Thanks for meeting with me."

He raised a hand, not looking at her. His eyes stayed glued to the papers.

"I have a lot of grading ahead of me tonight," he said. "I would appreciate it if we could make this quick."

"Of course," said Jasmine. She dragged a seat over to his desk and sat down.

Sampson stared at her through his tiny glasses. He sighed and abandoned his busy work, taking a seat, leaning forward with his elbows on his bony knees.

"I think I've read enough mystery books to see where this is going," he said. "The bold young amateur sleuth, Jasmine Moore. And her sidekick Luffy. It just so happens that murder seems to follow you wherever you go. Life truly does imitate art."

She smiled. "And the sleuth always has a list of suspects to interview."

A TIMELY MURDER

"Alright, Poirot," he said, gesturing as though to give her the floor. "Let's hear it."

"Well..." Jasmine touched a few discarded bits of paper that sat at the edge of the desk, fiddling with their crinkled edges. "Originally I wasn't even going to talk to you. Oliver wasn't even in any of your class periods, was he?"

Sampson shook his head. "No. But I'm curious... what made you decide to involve me?"

"Let's just call it intuition," said Jasmine. "A feeling."

Sampson smiled. "I'm familiar with that. Feeling and intuition. They seem like such pure, simple things when we read about them in books. But in real life they can be a lot trickier, can't they?"

She shrugged. "We'll see. Did you know Oliver at all?"

"No, I didn't know him personally."

"Personally?"

"I mean, I knew of him. He was the new president of the student council and he was making waves for a little while."

"What kind of waves?" Jasmine asked.

Sampson shrugged. "That's not really my area. All I care about is that I have tenure here, and I get to keep spreading the joy of creativity to future writers. As far as the future of Wildwood... I'm not worried."

"Why? Because it's been here for so long?"

Sampson chuckled. "I guess that is a kind of cognitive bias, isn't it? Just because something's old, we sometimes assume it'll be around forever. But sometimes the opposite is true. If something's old, it may be as close to death as it's ever been. That being said, I leave the changing of policies and methods to other people."

"So, you really don't know what Oliver was going after? You must have heard something, right?"

"I know he was going on about assigned parking," Sampson replied. Then, it seemed like inspiration came to him. A sudden thought, glowing in his eyes. "I think I also heard something about structural repairs. He wasn't happy with the state of some of the infrastructure around here."

"Like the railing from the clock tower?" Jasmine asked.

"Perhaps."

"Is there anything else you can tell me about Oliver?"

"Not off the top of my head," said Sampson. "Sorry. Like I said, I never knew him personally."

Jasmine nodded, holding in a sigh of frustration. A dead end, an intuition proven false. She thought she was quite skilled at detecting lies, and Sampson seemed to be telling the truth.

"One last question," she said. "I'm looking for someone. Kind of a friend of mine. He might have had a run-on with Oliver's dad. Do you know Lyle Bridges at all?"

"No," Sampson said quickly. "I don't know him. I've never been to Pineapple. I'm not a fan of that sort of food. You pay a hundred dollars and you don't even get full. What's the point?"

He laughed, shaking his head.

"I see what you mean," Jasmine replied. "My budget lets me get pizza once a week. That's about as fancy as I get."

"I know how that goes," Sampson said. "The life of a student can seem scary, Jasmine. But you'll look back on these years fondly. Don't waste them."

It was obviously meant as advice, but the tone of his voice made it feel more like a warning. Jasmine left the class room feeling strange.

"He was lying about Lyle," she said.

"How can you tell?" Luffy asked.

"The way his voice changed. He couldn't wait to change the subject. I'm not sure if it has anything to do with Oliver, but he's definitely hiding something."

The next stop was the class commonly called LnL, the language and linguistics course. She found the door already open, held by a rubber door stop. Alan Keller was inside, lounging on the hardwood stage beside his desk. He was holding something up to the light, staring through it with one eye closed. When Jasmine came closer, she saw that it was a ring. A wedding ring, it seemed, and a rather fancy one as well. Gold band, a huge rock catching the light and refracting it in scintillating patterns.

"Is that yours?" she asked.

Keller coughed once, sitting up and smoothing down his wild, wispy hair. He looked at her, holding up his other hand, which was marked by a plain silver band.

"I have mine right here," he said. "I found this one on my desk last week, along with a note. I thought nothing of it at the time, but..."

"A note?" Jasmine asked. "Can I see it?"

He nodded, scooting across the floor to grab a scrap of paper off the corner of his desk. He handed it over.

The handwriting was unfamiliar to Jasmine, but it was messy, clumsy, and smudged, which made her assume it was the scrawl of a male person.

I don't know how to figure out this mess I'm in. Hopefully someone will come along who does. Hold on to this for me. I can't trust anyone else right now.

"Professor," Jasmine said, her heart thumping. "We need to figure out who wrote this. We need to-"

"Compare handwriting?" he offered. "I thought of that. You can blame the digital age for my failings. Just about every paper I have is typed and printed."

"Then let me take it," Jasmine said. "I can bring it to the police. They'll be able to identify the writer. But they also may need a statement from you."

Keller shrugged. "Sure. I don't mind."

"Okay. Do you have a bag? Anything I can store this in?"

Keller got off the floor with a chorus of grunts and popping joints. He limped around to the front of his desk and pulled a sandwich bag out of one of the drawers.

"I used these for that little role-playing game we played in class a few weeks ago," he said. "The only thing that's ever been stored in it is paper. Take it."

She slid both the ring and the note inside the baggie, sealed it up, and put it into her backpack.

"Do you think Oliver could have written it?" she asked.

"It would make sense," said Keller. "He apparently was in some sort of trouble, or else he wouldn't have ended up... you know. I wish I would have done more, but I had no idea who might have written that note until Oliver was found."

"Well," said Jasmine, "I wish you wouldn't have handled the ring with your bare hands."

"It was too late, anyhow. The only reason I saw it on my desk was because some student came up to ask me a question and started fiddling with it. Whatever evidence was on there is ruined now."

Jasmine nodded. "Do you remember who this student was?"

Keller narrowed his eyes, staring toward the ceiling. His tongue darted around for a moment as he tried to recall.

"Oh, yes," he said at last. "It was that friend of yours, Charles Dane. He wanted to know... well, some such question about the course work. I can't rightly recall."

Jasmine stared at Luffy. He stared back. They were beginning to see that this could very well be the type of mess that Oliver had found himself embroiled in.

Chapter 13

"The evidence is leading us around in circles," Jasmine said as they walked through the quiet halls. "I thought we'd eliminate a few suspects today, but instead we just keep shifting suspicion around. It's like a game of spin the bottle, or something."

"What's spin the bottle?" Luffy asked.

"It's a game where you... well, you sit in a circle with a bunch of people and spin a bottle. Whoever it's pointing at when it stops, you have to kiss that person."

"What does that have to do with solving Oliver's murder?" Luffy asked with genuine curiosity, as though he was missing some brilliant piece of deduction.

"It's just an analogy. In this case, whoever the bottle's pointing at is the killer. It keeps moving around."

"Oh. I get it. But maybe we should play spin the bottle some time. I'll kiss anyone, I don't care."

"I know you don't, buddy," she said, ruffling the fur on his back. "But this is a different kind of kissing?"

"Oh! You mean, it's that weird kind that Brandon wanted to do with you. And now Charles wants it too."

She stared at him, making a disgusted face. "Charles?"

"Jeez, maybe I'm the real detective here. They should change the billing around. It's not Jaz and Luffy anymore. Now it's Luffy and Jaz."

She groaned. "Just tell me what you're talking about."

"Do I have to spell it out?" Luffy asked. "I guess I do. Well, my brilliant friend, just earlier today Charles says he wanted Alicia's help hooking him up with a girl he liked. Then when you asked him about it he got all cagey."

"Did he get cagey?" Jasmine asked. "Maybe we're remembering it differently."

"Oh, he got cagey alright."

She shrugged. "I think that's just the way he is."

"Yeah, well, that is true. But it's also true that he likes you."

Jasmine sighed. "Boys and their crushes. I think we do need to talk to him again, but I'm not bringing this up."

"We need to know about the ring, right?" Luffy asked.

Jasmine nodded. "Charles is smart. If both he and that ring have something to do with Oliver's death, I wouldn't be surprised if he spotted it and decided to try and mess up the evidence somehow. It's a long shot, but it's possible."

"You could probably say the same thing about his chances with you."

"Shut up, Luffy."

He barked at her in response, but said nothing more.

They found Professor Lucille Whitaker hard at work on her computer, typing fast and frowning in concentration. She was the youngest tenured professor in all of Wildwood's history, and it showed. Jasmine thought Lucille looked younger than she did in a lot of ways, perhaps owing to the glow of pregnancy.

Normally, Lucille was a calm, patient, and all-round lovely individual. Jasmine was surprised when the professor didn't even look at her as she came in, instead raising a finger to instruct her to wait. She then went back to typing without a word, her frown deepening. She seemed frustrated by something. Angry, even.

Jasmine licked her lips. "Professor Whitaker, I-"

"Not a problem!" Lucille said a voice that sounded quite fake. She smiled now, but still did not take her eyes from the screen. "Just a moment."

She typed a few more words, clicked a few times, then switched her monitor off. Turning toward Jasmine, she sat in her usual patient posture. But today it seemed affected rather than genuine, as if she was straining toward normalcy.

"I can come back another time if it's more convenient," Jasmine said.

"No, don't bother with that," said Lucille. "I just want you to know something, Jasmine. Mothers are very protective of their children. Even the ones who aren't born yet."

"I'm sure they are," Jasmine replied, narrowing her eyes. "My mother worries about me all the time."

Lucille nodded. "If I was her, I'd do the same. I don't appreciate what you're doing. Not at all."

"Oh?" Jasmine asked, feeling a flame of anger curling up inside her. "What is it I'm doing that's bothering you so much?"

"You're bringing me into something I have no reason to be a part of. I don't consent to being a suspect in your sad little amateur investigation. If you don't mind me saying, I think whatever success you had before has now gone completely to your head."

Luffy growled, folding back his ears. Lucille jumped back, staring at him with fear in her eyes.

"Don't worry about him," Jasmine said. "He's never bitten anyone. Not even the murderer I helped catch in Blackwood Cove. And he won't bite the murderer I'm going to catch here, either. And you can't just verbally abuse me like that."

Lucille reeled herself back in toward the desk. Her formerly perfect hair had started to fall apart. Strands of it had come loose from the ponytail and now trailed across her forehead.

"Actually, I can," she said. "I have a family, Miss Moore. And I'm going to say this once. Don't mess with my family, whatever you do."

Jasmine's jaw dropped. "Your family? Who said anything about them?"

"You don't understand. How could you? If you mess with me, you mess with them. It really is that simple. My babies need me and I'm not going to get into trouble because some girl with delusions of grandeur decided I was involved with something."

"Miss Whitaker," Jasmine said patiently. "That's not what this is about. I just wanted to ask you some questions, since you were one of Oliver's teachers. And because I thought you were a bit more open-minded than this."

Lucille pulled her hair out of the ponytail with a grunt of irritation and set to fixing it. "You can ask your questions. I won't stop you. It's your right to talk."

"Okay, then. Did anything happen recently with Oliver? Any change in his behavior? Anything strange at all?"

"Yeah, actually. His grades started to drop. The quality of his work went down. I noticed he seemed a little distracted in class. I figured it was because of his position on the student council. That sort of thing tends to steal your attention."

Jasmine nodded. "Did he seem... worried? Troubled?"

Lucille shook her head. "No. But that doesn't mean he wasn't. Oliver was like a turtle... when he wanted to be safe, he pulled back in his shell."

Jasmine opened her backpack and pulled out the baggie she had gotten from Professor Keller.

"Does this ring look familiar to you?" she asked.

As Lucille looked, Jasmine paid close attentions to the woman's face. Especially the eyes. No matter what came out of her mouth, the real answer would be shown in the small, involuntary movements in her facial muscles.

"No, I don't think so," Lucille said. "A bit gaudy for my tastes. You can't do anything when you've got a stone that big sticking out from your finger."

Jasmine looked down at Luffy and nodded, as though to say she gets a pass.

Then she turned the bag around and showed Lucille what was behind the ring; the note that Keller had found.

"Do you recognize this handwriting?" she asked.

"Should I?" said Lucille.

"Maybe. Maybe not. I was just wondering if you might have recognized it."

Lucille studied it for a moment, frowning again. Then she shook her head.

"It could be any number of students," she said. "They all have terrible handwriting. Laptops and printers were God's gift to teachers around the world."

Lucille attempted a smile then, and mostly succeeded. Jasmine stared, trying to figure out what was going on behind the young professor's pearly white teeth and gorgeous green eyes. Pregnancy hormones playing havoc with her emotional state, or something else? Either way, she seemed to be trying to smooth things over, to end the conversation on a peaceful note.

"Is there anything else you can think of that could be of importance?" Jasmine asked coldly, refusing to climb back up on the high road now that she had been dragged down off it.

"That depends," said Lucille.

"On what?"

"On whether or not you've already talked to Alan Keller."

Jasmine leaned forward. "Why would you bring his name up?"

Lucille smiled. "So, you have talked to him. Maybe you should try again. What did he tell you, that Oliver was a model student? That no one hated him? Well, I can tell you one person who did hate him."

"Keller?" Jasmine said. "Why? How?"

"Because Mr. Bridges was a know-it-all," Lucille said. "There's nothing wrong with that. I was the same when I was in school. Don't tell me you haven't noticed."

Jasmine thought back. She could remember a number of times when Oliver spoke out of turn in LnL, correcting the professor or offering expansions on whatever Keller was attempting to explain.

"Keller always seemed fine with it," she said.

"Because he's old and wise and knows when to hold and when to fold," said Lucille. "But I've heard him ranting in the lounge between classes. Complaining how that Bridges kid was undermining him in class and how he wished Oliver would just go away."

Jasmine nodded, leaning back in her chair. Collapsing. This was getting more confused by the moment.

"This is off the record, by the way," said Lucille. "If I see my words in print somewhere..."

For punctuation to her unfinished threat, the professor smiled and reached across the table to tap Jasmine on the hand.

Jasmine didn't consider herself an angry person, but it took all her willpower to say "thank you" and not to kick the woman in the shins as she shot to her feet and left the room. She hadn't even been able to get to half her questions, such as who was the man Jasmine had seen her with outside the ice cream parlor, the man who was often seen wandering around campus? Most likely he was her husband, but Jasmine had a strange feeling about the whole thing.

"I kind of hope she does turn out to be the killer," Luffy said when they were in the hall. "It couldn't happen to a nastier person."

Jasmine shrugged. "Don't mess with mama bear, I guess. I hope she isn't the killer, because if she is I'll have to talk to her again at some point."

"But if she isn't, you'll have to keep going to her class," Luffy reminded her.

"Dang it. You're right. Is it too late in the semester to drop her course?"

"How should I know?" Luffy asked. "I'm a dog. But you could just stop showing up. Like Alicia."

"That reminds me..."

Jasmine took out her phone and checked her notifications. Still nothing from Alicia. There was a text from Charles, however.

Heads up. I heard some things outside of class just after lunch today. I think someone has it out for you, but I don't know who.

Jasmine drew her head back, blinking her eyes a few times. She tried scrolling down, but the message ended there. There was nothing else.

She began to type out a reply, asking for an explanation. She kept walking, heading back toward Keller's room.

She was nearly there when the door of the classroom banged open and several people stepped out. Jasmine looked up, seeing blue uniforms and badges. At the front of the group was Luke Barrett, looking like a man at a funeral. Behind them was Alan Keller, staring around in confusion.

"There she is," one of the other officers said.

Jasmine stopped in her tracks as the police marched toward her.

"Jasmine Moore," Barrett said with a sigh. "I'm afraid I'm going to have to arrest you under suspicion of the murder of Oliver Bridges. You have the right to remain silent..."

Chapter 14

"Did not see that one coming," said Luffy.

Jasmine stared out through the bars, her eyes wide and unfocused. She sat perfectly still on a cot that looked like it was made of some kind of padded material but felt like it was made out of cement. And that same cement seemed to be encasing her soul, crushing it, smothering her under a suffocating weight. A few days ago, she had everything figured out. The future. The course her life was taking. Now nothing made sense. It was as if she had taken a wrong turn at some point and ended up in a parallel universe.

"What happened?" she asked.

Luffy had no answer for her. He padded back over from his spot by the wall and sat between her legs, resting his chin on her thigh and staring up at her with sad eyes.

"What are you thinking about?" he asked.

"I'm trying to figure out who I can trust," Jasmine said.

"With what?"

She tried to smile. "Just because I'm down and out, doesn't mean you have to be. I can survive in here for a little while, but you can't."

"Sure I can!" he said, yipping fearfully.

"Not unless you learn how to use a toilet."

"Jasmine, no! I won't leave! You can't make me."

"I could call mom and dad. Or I could call Brandon. Someone from home. They could come get you. It's a long drive, but they'll make it in a heartbeat."

Out in the corridor, there was a metal clanging sound, followed by footsteps. A tired looking female officer appeared, holding a cup of coffee and a set of keys.

"Jasmine Moore," she said. "You have a phone call waiting."

She jumped up and rushed for the bars. The officer pulled the cell open and let her through, cuffing her hands in front of her and giving Luffy a warning glance.

Following the officer through the station house, passing some familiar areas on the way, she came to a bank of phones. One of them had a blinking light on, it signifying a call waiting.

"You can take it here," the officer said. "You can make another call afterwards, if you want."

Jasmine nodded, waiting for the cop to back away a bit before lifting the receiver to her ear.

"Hello?" she said.

There was a heavy sigh, followed by a familiar voice.

"Jasmine," Sheriff Kenneth Lustbader said. "I heard through the grapevine that you got in a spot of trouble out there. What in the world is going on?"

"Sheriff, it's awesome to hear your voice," she said. "You have to help me. You can, right? I didn't do anything."

"Calm down, Jasmine. Just take a deep breath. Obviously I know you didn't do anything. What's been going on?"

She explained everything to him as best she could with her shaking voice and the looming presence of the officer nearby.

"I guess I'm probably about to tell you something you already know," Lustbader said at the end, "but you're not in Blackwood Cove. You're in a big place with different rules. You've got to take care of yourself. I think you need to abandon this case as soon as you get out of jail."

"I was afraid you were going to say that," Jasmine replied.

"And I was afraid of hearing that usual stubbornness in your voice. I guess I can't convince you to do anything, can I? I learned that lesson already. Have they told you what they have you for?"

"Just that I'm under suspicion. They haven't given me any details."

"Then they'll have to be doing that pretty soon, here. Maybe it's not as bad as you're probably afraid it is. Just a precautionary thing, like how we nabbed Randy Ballard before. Look, I'm going to try and do my best to help out. I don't have much pull, but we both know someone who does."

"Marlon," Jasmine said.

"Yeah. If I can get hold of him, which is doubtful. But I wouldn't be surprised if he's been keeping tabs on you. Don't worry, Jasmine. Everything'll be fine."

"I'm sure it will be," she said glumly.

"How's old Luffy doing?"

Jasmine looked down at him. "Right now, he's pretty much surgically attached to my leg."

"Yeah, I'll bet. Tell him I said you'll both be out of there real soon. It won't mean much to him, but I'll feel better if you tell him. I dunno... sometimes I get the feeling there's more to Luffy than we know."

Jasmine suppressed her laughter. "Yeah. I get that feeling sometimes, too."

"Well, take care Jasmine. Do you want to let your folks know, or should I?"

"I'm about to do it as soon as I get off the phone with you," Jasmine replied.

"Okay. Bye, then. And remember your rights. Don't let them bully you around."

She tried to imagine Luke Barrett bullying anyone and failed.

The phone clicked, telling her Lustbader had hung up. Jasmine took a few deep breaths, reached out to start dialing her house back in Blackwood Cove, and chickened out at the last second. Several further attempts ended with the same result. Finally, on the fifth try, she managed to make her fingers do the right thing.

"Mom," she said when the phone was answered. "Something happened, and it isn't my fault..."

As she explained things, and listened to her mother's response, relief flooded through her. When she hung up, she didn't feel much different about her chances of getting out of jail. But she was glad to know that she and Luffy wouldn't be alone for long. Her parents were going to start driving as soon as they could, but they had to wait for their car to be finished at the mechanic. They would be in New Market sometime in the next twenty-four hours.

As soon as the phone was back on its cradle, the same officer approached from behind. The coffee cup was gone, and the woman looked more awake now. And also more prone to getting angry, so Jasmine went along without a word.

But she wasn't led back to her cell. Instead, she was brought to the same interrogation room she had been in once before. The door was shut and locked behind her, and Luke Barrett glanced at her over his shoulder.

"You're alone," Jasmine said.

"Why shouldn't I be?" Barrett asked.

She shrugged. "I thought you were supposed to have another person in here, at least until I was safely handcuffed to the table."

He shook his head. "There's no need for that though. Right? You can sit down. I'd like to go through some things with you."

He reached into his lap, and Jasmine heard a sound of crinkling plastic. Barrett pulled a few dog treats out of a bag and set them on the table.

"For Luffy," he said. "I don't know if you like to make him do a trick first, or what?"

The dog licked his chops, staring toward the table. For the first time in the past hour, he was not overwhelmed with fear and anxiety.

Jasmine shuffled around to her side of the table and pulled out the chair with her handcuffed hands. Sitting down, she grabbed a treat and tossed it toward the floor. It never made it there, and a second later Luffy was staring at her waiting for more.

"I never thought I'd be wearing a set of cuffs," Jasmine said. "Not for real, anyway. In fourth grade a cop came into our class and we all got to try some on. It was a lot different than this."

Barrett chuckled. "Because your wrists were so much smaller, huh?"

She shook her head. "Because I didn't feel like a criminal. I didn't feel dirty for no reason. What's this all about, Luke?"

He couldn't meet her eyes. He moved around in his chair like the seat was getting either very hot or very cold.

"Look, I'm sorry," he said. "I like you Jasmine. Heck, I respect you. But I can't ignore evidence, not even when it points to someone I care for."

Jasmine pointed to a yellow envelope on the table. "I guess this is where that comes in."

He nodded, pulling on a pair of disposable gloves. He opened the envelope and tipped it out into his hand. A small plastic bag fell out, containing an object Jasmine recognized immediately.

It was square, leathery, with a couple of small holes in the middle. It had a conspicuous marking on it, a heart drawn in with permanent marker; a parting gift from her mother, a reminder of the love they shared.

It was the small diamond-shaped patch from her backpack. Just one of those doohickeys which she didn't know the purpose of. She hadn't even realized it was missing from her bag.

"This was found at the top of the clock tower," Barrett said. "We've had it in evidence ever since the day Oliver died, but it wasn't until earlier today that we were able to figure out where it was from. You know what this thing is, don't you?"

She nodded. No point lying. That would only make her look guiltier.

Barrett nodded back. "We have your bag in lockup now. We were able to match this piece up with it. Jasmine, do you have any idea how or why this ended up on the clock tower?"

She shook her head. Meanwhile, her mind and body felt like they were being pulled down a sink hole. Surely, this could not be her reality. It was all some big prank.

"I haven't been on the clock tower since initiation," she said. "I always wanted to go back up, but I guess I never found the time."

"I believe you," said Barrett. "But there's no proof that you're telling the truth."

"And there's no proof that I'm not," she said. "If you have a witness, then they're obviously lying."

She felt something wet against her arm. Looking down, she saw Luffy staring up at her with begging eyes. She threw him another treat; he turned around and chased it across the small room.

"We don't have a witness," Barrett admitted.

"Good. How about this patch from my bag? How did you know it was mine?"

"An anonymous source. We can't give out the identity of the person, Jasmine. You understand, right?"

"I understand that we're wasting our time," said Jasmine. "We both know I didn't kill Oliver."

"But knowing is half the battle. We have to prove beyond a reasonable doubt that you couldn't have done it."

Jasmine threw herself back in her chair, howling with anger.

"Sorry," Barrett said.

"So, I'm just a suspect now?" she asked. "Is that it? You asked me to help you, and that was what I was trying to do. Now look what has happened! You want the information I've been able to gather or what?"

Barrett nodded. "It would be helpful."

Jasmine smiled nastily. "Yeah, and it would be helpful to not be in jail. But that's just too bad, huh?"

"So, you're not going to tell me?"

"Not until I'm free?"

Barrett winced. "Jasmine, there's no need to be petty."

"But pettiness is all I have left. You brought this on yourself, Barrett. I suggest you get to work on trying to exonerate me, or else your case on Oliver Bridges isn't going anywhere."

Barrett shook his head. "Jasmine, think of the boy's parents. Think of their pain. Do you really want to hold back information?"

She nodded, steeling herself. She set her jaw and made her eyes go cold. It was a flimsy bluff. Anyone who had known her longer than a week or two would know she had no intention of messing up the investigation. But Barrett didn't know that, and maybe it would light a fire under his butt. Maybe it would get her out of here in time. And if not... then she would just have to spill the beans.

As far as Barrett went, she felt terrible about manipulating him. He was a good man, and a good cop. He could have easily threatened her with a charge of interfering with an investigation, but he didn't even bring it up.

"I guess this is one of those stalemates, huh?" he said.

"I guess so."

"There's nothing I can do to convince you?"

She fed Luffy the last treat and didn't answer.

Chapter 15

"You have a visitor."

Jasmine looked up from her depressed stupor and saw Joe Sanderson standing there outside her cell, his slender fingers wrapped around the bars. She stood up and moved toward him.

"Joe!" she said. "I was hoping you would show up."

He smiled. "I tried finding you at Wildwood. Some old bald guy told me you were in here."

"Keller," said Jasmine. "Did he say anything else? Was he acting weird?"

Joe shrugged. "Sorry. I don't have the same eye for people that you do."

He was right, in a literal way. Even now, he could barely meet her eyes. She thought that was some part of him was still locked away in a private little cave of his own making. Perhaps even the majority of him.

"Why are you here?" Jasmine asked.

"I thought you might want some help," he replied. "I don't know what, but I'd feel pretty bad if I didn't come."

Jasmine sighed. "Thanks, Joe. No one else has come."

He smiled a little at that. "Now that I'm here, I guess I don't really know what I'm supposed to say. Or do. Tell me, Jasmine. Please. You helped me out a lot. Now you need my help, and there's nothing..."

Jasmine touched his hand where it was wrapped around the bars.

"There are two things you can do," she said. "And I promise they'll be enough. You don't have to keep feeling like you owe me anything, Joe. I brought you with me to New Market so you could have a second chance, not so I could have someone who's constantly beholden to me."

He nodded slowly. "Okay. I understand. What are the two things?"

Jasmine eyed the officer, who was standing about eight feet away. Still well within range of hearing, but the woman was back to looking bored and tired. A cup of coffee or a nap were probably the chief thoughts in her mind. It was doubtful she had any interest in what the detainee and her visitor were talking about, so long as no physical altercation took place.

"You can tell me what happened between you and Lyle Bridges," Jasmine said.

It was a crapshoot. All she knew was that Joe had made some kind of scene at Pineapple; whether or not it involved Lyle directly was up in the air. But she desperately wanted to start putting some pieces of the puzzle together, for her sanity if for no other reason.

Joe looked at the floor. "How did you hear about that?"

"Officer Barrett," said Jasmine. "He heard a tip from the restaurant."

"I don't want to get in trouble," Joe replied. "I doubt they would take it very easy on me in here. I don't think most people see me as human, Jasmine."

"But I do, and you're telling me. So, what happened?"

He sighed. "I went in to ask for a job. The hostess sort of chuckled at me. She looked at me like I was a sideshow act, or something. She did hand me an application, but her attitude told me not to bother."

"Let me guess," Luffy said. "You bothered."

Joe continued a moment later of his own accord. "I came back with the application half an hour later. I had fixed my hair, changed my clothes out for a set that wasn't so dirty. I thought maybe they would take pity on me. The hostess wasn't there, but a man in a suit was standing at the counter helping a server with drinks. I waited until he wasn't so busy, then I handed my application over and thanked him."

"Was this man Lyle Bridges?" Jasmine asked.

Joe nodded. "I saw his nametag, but it didn't mean anything to me. As you can probably imagine, I'm a bit behind on current events. I could obviously see that Pineapple was a nice place, but I had no idea it was some kind of world class establishment."

"I assume he rejected you," said Jasmine.

"He did more than that," Joe replied, his grip tightening on the bars of the cell. "He told me the hostess had made a mistake in handing me an application. He balled it up and threw it in the trash and told me to leave. Guess what I did next? You probably want to say I ran away. But I didn't do that. I got angry. Angrier than I've been in years. It wasn't the first time I'd been turned down, but Lyle was the only one to do it so bluntly. Maybe I should have respected that. Maybe I should have been glad he didn't get my hopes up. Obviously no place wants to hire someone like me."

"Someone will eventually," Jasmine said.

"I don't know about that," said Joe. "Sometimes I think I made a mistake, coming back to civilization. Like I'm a different animal, and this isn't the place for me. And sometimes I think everyone out here in the world is a lot nastier than they have any logical reason to be. They're just nasty for the sake of it, because it makes them feel better about themselves or whatever.

"And all those thoughts were running through my mind as I stood there, staring at Lyle. I guess he could probably tell I was getting mad, because he took a step back, using the counter as a shield. But I didn't try and hit him, or anything. I just started yelling. I yelled about how selfish he was, how mean and nasty, how other people had given him all this success with their generosity but he couldn't be bothered to spread any of that back. Everyone in the restaurant was staring. The hostess and all the other workers were watching from afar. Lyle listened to my whole tirade, and then he picked up the phone. 'I'm going to call the police,' he said, 'if you don't get out of here right now!' So I left, finally. I got a bit of sense back in my brain and left. But not before I said one of the dumbest things I've ever said."

"What was it?" Jasmine asked.

"I told Lyle that one day he'd be sorry," Joe replied, hanging his head even further. "I told him I'd make sure of it."

Jasmine sighed. "That does sound bad, Joe."

"I know, but I didn't mean it like that. I just meant that I'd become successful and rich too, just like he is, and I'd teach him not to judge people so fast. That's all I meant."

"I'm sure of that," said Jasmine. "The cops probably know all these details by now. They must have called that person at Pineapple back."

Joe nodded. "They already questioned me. I explained everything. I don't know what they're going to do with it."

"Probably nothing," said Jasmine. "Not while I'm still in here. They have a piece of evidence on me, Joe. Real, material evidence. What you did doesn't outweigh that. I want you to tell me one more thing... was Oliver at the restaurant that day?"

Joe nodded. "He was there, sitting at the bar. Looked like he had just gotten there. He was doing homework, I think, with his headphones on. But he took them off when I started yelling. When I left... he followed me out. I could hear his father yelling for him to come back, but Oliver ignored him. He caught up to me, and he told me to be careful who I messed with."

"He threatened you?" Jasmine asked.

"No. He didn't make it sound like a threat. More like a warning, like he was on my side. Then he went back in."

"What did you do next?"

"I came to your place," he said with a shaky smile. "That was the day you found me at your door, remember?"

Jasmine nodded. It was starting to come together now, in the faintest of ways. The skeleton of the problem was still mostly bare, but some wisps of flesh were beginning to form around the peripheries.

"That's all I wanted to talk about," she said. "Unless there's anything else you can think of that I'd like to know."

Joe shook his head. "I've been avoiding the area around Pineapple like the plague since that day. Too much shame. I felt terrible about my outburst, especially after what happened to Oliver... for no real reason, I just felt like I had made one of his final days less pleasant than it could have been. I thought of visiting you at Wildwood a couple of times, but I was too afraid of who I might run into."

"You could have visited my apartment again," Jasmine said.

He shrugged. "I don't know why I didn't. I don't know why I'm like this."

"Because you're you," said Jasmine. "If everyone was the same, life would be boring. Listen... my apartment is empty now. Obviously. Barrett will give you my key, I'm sure. Someone has to take care of Luffy. I was keeping him with me until someone showed up who could take him."

Joe and Luffy shared a look. The dog flicked his tail nervously. They had a working relationship. They were acquaintances, but maybe they could be more.

"For how long?" Joe asked.

"No more than twenty-four hours," she replied. "My parents will be here by then."

Joe nodded. "I can do that. You can count on it, Jasmine."

And so Luffy was gone. For the first time in many months, Jasmine was fully alone. Always he had been there, even weaseling his way into the bathroom whenever she wanted privacy, or waiting just outside the door. He was there in the morning when she opened her eyes, staring patiently and waiting for her to wake up or else snoozing right along with her.

And now he was gone.

Jasmine didn't know what to do with herself. She felt shame, burning hot inside her. Sadness. She felt like the worst person in the world for sending him away, and she kept remembering the way he looked back at her as Joe led him down the hall. He had gone, but not willingly. Even now, she felt like he had left something of himself in the cell with her. He would never be free until she was.

But she knew she had done the right thing. She would be with him again soon.

There was nothing to do now but sit and wait for something to happen.

Finally, two hours after Luffy had disappeared, Barrett appeared outside her cell. He was wearing an apologetic smile, and holding a greasy paper bag.

"I brought you some food," he said. "I know you like cheeseburgers and fries. Maybe we can talk a bit more."

Jasmine stood up, shaking off her stupor. Barrett unlocked the cell and they walked together back to the same old interrogation room. This time Jasmine wasn't put in cuffs. All the better to dig into her fast food treat, which she did not hesitate to do. The only time she slowed down was when she reflexively reached under the table to feed Luffy a few fries... only to remember that he wasn't there. She let out a quiet sigh and went back to her burger.

"Thirsty?" Barrett asked, sliding a frosty can of cola over to her. "A bit of caffeine and sugar for ya. Nothing better, right?"

She popped open the can and took a long, frosty swallow. She felt the cold, acidic tang creeping down her throat. After hours of stale cell air and warm tap water to drink, it seemed like the greatest thing ever.

"I was just wondering," Barrett said casually, as though it were a side matter of little importance, "if you'd given the evidence any more thought. The patch from your backpack. Maybe you remember how it ended up there."

"I wish I did," she said. "But I have no idea."

He nodded. "Yeah, I've got nothing concrete either. Obviously there's more than one way. It could have fallen off your pack and someone dragged it up there on the bottom of their shoe. Or maybe it was planted there by someone who wanted you to go down."

"That could be," said Jasmine. "But I know one way that couldn't have happened. I didn't go up there. I haven't been up there in a long time."

Barrett nodded. "We figured out that Oliver died the night before he was found. He was cold and stiff when we brought him into the lab. He'd been there for at least ten hours, maybe longer. Which means he fell off that tower when at least a few stragglers must have been at Wildwood. There could be a witness that isn't coming forward for some reason. Someone who could exonerate you."

"Or condemn me," Jasmine said with a smile.

"Not if you didn't do it."

"I didn't."

"Then I guess it's all settled between us," said Barrett. "We just have to let the evidence catch up. Hang in there, Jasmine. I'm not sure if you do anymore, but I still have faith in our procedures."

"That's good for you, Barrett. I've had to give up my freedom, and now my dog. Pretty soon I feel like I might need to give up my crappy jail cell for an even crappier prison cell. I'm getting railroaded here. It happens all the time. You know it does. An incompetent police force can't actually solve a crime, so they latch onto the first suspect who comes along. And an innocent person goes down for something they didn't do."

Barrett nodded. "It does happen. But it won't happen to you. Not while I'm around."

Jasmine smiled. "I see you aren't holding my past words against me."

His eyes went wide. "What words?"

"You know... me holding back evidence in exchange for freedom."

"That?" Barrett said with a smile. "It's up to you what you tell us, Jasmine. But if you know something that might be able to get you out of hot water..."

"That all depends on how much stock your colleagues will put in what I say," Jasmine replied with a shrug.

Barrett shook his head. "I'm still in charge of this investigation, Jasmine. I have more power than they do. Are you sure there isn't anything you want to tell me?"

Jasmine thought about that slowly. She thought about it long and hard as she ate the rest of her food, nibbling away at it gradually. Barrett sat patiently, wordlessly, and watched her. He didn't seem to be in any hurry. Not at first glance. But there was a certain harried look in his eyes that Jasmine only noticed when she looked deeply into him. His knee kept bouncing up and down. He was worried.

In the end, she decided to come forward. So it began, a spilling forth of all the confused knowledge she had gathered. Barrett listened closely, leaning forward on the table like an attentive student.

Chapter 16

"Listen here, Joe," Luffy said. "We've got stuff to do, and it doesn't involve sitting around here feeling sad and pathetic."

The drifter just sat there in the recliner, staring into space, his hand idly scratching Luffy's neck. This wasn't going anywhere. Time was being wasted.

Luffy broke away and went to the door, jumping up to put his forepaws on it, nosing the leash that hung on a nearby hook.

"Look, dummy," Luffy said. "I want to go for a walk. Look here! Obviously I can't talk to you, but I'm sure you can read between the lines here."

Joe glanced up, frowning for a moment, then shifting forward at last in the chair.

"You want to go out?" he asked.

Luffy barked. "Obviously! What's it look like?"

He didn't think it was possible to miss Jasmine more than he already did, but this guy was starting to prove him wrong.

Joe finally got up. With a long-suffering sigh he pulled his shoes on, then grabbed the leash and hooked it to Luffy's neck.

"Hey," Luffy said. "The man can learn. Good. Now let's go!"

Evidently, Joe thought they were just going for a routine potty break. But Luffy immediately started pulling the poor guy along, yanking and clawing his way through the grass and across the asphalt.

"Whoa!" Joe called. "Hold on!"

"No," said Luffy. "You hold on. I'm on a mission, and you aren't going to be able to stop me."

As soon as they were out on the sidewalk, Luffy put his nose to the pavement and started sniffing along. He knew the scent he was looking for, and it was only a matter of time before he found it.

"Jasmine?"

She heard her name from somewhere up above, beyond what was currently happening. It was like the voice of God shouting down at her, echoing through heaven and sky to reach her where she was, far down...

It was dark. It was cold and damp. She felt her clothing stick to her and her breath rushing in and out in gasping torrents. She was running up winding stone steps, past narrow windows filled with old, yellow glass. It was the clock tower at Wildwood. She was trying to reach the top... and there was someone up ahead of her. Someone behind her, too.

"Jasmine!"

She came back. She awoke in the interrogation room, slumped back in her chair but with her hands gripping the edge of the table hard, as though it was a lifeline in a stormy sea. She sat forward quickly, clearing her throat and stretching her neck, playing it off.

"Are you OK?" Barrett asked, with a shocked expression on his face. "I thought I lost you for a second."

"Hm?" She stared at him.

"It looked like you were having some kind of seizure," Barrett replied.

"Oh, that?" She smiled. "It's just something that happens to me now and then. It's stress induced. It's been happening my whole life. My doctor told me it's nothing to worry about."

"But what if you fell?" Barrett asked.

"I never have," said Jasmine. "It's nothing."

She drank down the last of her soda, taking her time, hoping Barrett would move on. The last thing she wanted was to be checked into a hospital somewhere. But he didn't look like he was going to drop it. He looked concerned.

There was a knock at the door behind him. It opened a moment later, and another officer stuck his head in.

"You've got a call, Barrett," the man said. "It's important."

Barrett nodded and got to his feet. "I'll be right back, Jasmine. Don't go anywhere."

"Funny," she said.

Barrett smiled as he stepped into the hall. The door was shut and locked behind him. Even if it hadn't been locked, Jasmine wasn't about to try and escape. She already knew she was innocent, but a breakout attempt would land her back in her cell with new charges. Ones that would stick.

So she sat. While she was waiting, she cleaned up the area a bit. She wadded the burger wrapper into a ball, collapse the little cardboard sleeve that held the fries, and stuffed both into the paper bag along with the empty can. She scraped a few errant bits of onion off the tabletop and tossed those in as well. And then there was nothing else. Nothing left to occupy herself. She sat and stared at the door, willing it to open.

And finally it did. It swung halfway ajar, and Barrett stuck his head and shoulders into the room. His ruddy cheeks had gone quite a bit ruddier. He smiled, but it was a nervous kind of smile.

"Good news," he said. "You're getting out of here."

Jasmine hopped to her feet, tucking the fast food bag under her arm. "What? How?"

"I'll take you down to the desk and your things will be handed over," Barrett explained. "I'll give you a ride back home."

Jasmine followed him out into the hall. "Barrett, who called?"

He shook his head. "Sorry for this whole mix-up, Jasmine. If there's anything else I can do, just ask."

"It was an FBI agent, wasn't it?" she asked with a grin. "A guy named Marlon Gale?"

He said nothing, and gave nothing away.

At the front counter, Jasmine was given back all her things. Her phone, her wallet, and her backpack. Nothing was missing. She was certain everything had been gone through, but the police had found nothing they thought was worth keeping.

Jasmine and Barrett stepped out into a rainy evening. The streets looked like they had been subject to a recent downpour that was only just starting to peter out into a light sprinkle.

"Why won't you tell me who called?" she asked.

"Because they didn't want to be identified," said Barrett. He opened the front passenger door of his squad car, then stepped around to the other side.

Jasmine slipped into the front seat and pulled the door shut against the wind and rain. Beside her, Barrett turned on the engine and kicked the heat up a notch to dispel the wet chill in the air. But he didn't disengage the car from park. He simply gripped the gear shift in one hand and the steering wheel in the other, chewing his lip as he stared out through a windshield smeared with rain.

"Motive is the question," he said.

Jasmine turned her whole body toward him, waiting.

"We know a few people who might have had a reason to kill Oliver," she added.

Barrett nodded, turning a knob to switch the wipers on at their lowest setting. "There's your friend, Charles Dane. Oliver beat him out for a position he badly wanted, right? Then there's Professor Keller. Oliver undermined him in class and made him feel dumb. It's a flimsy reason to kill someone, but I've seen flimsier. Who else?"

"Dean DuPont," Jasmine said. "Oliver was trying to change things at Wildwood, and he was making the whole school board look bad."

"Is that it?" Barrett asked.

"Those are the definite suspects," said Jasmine. "I have some suspicions about Lucille Whitaker. She was way too defensive when I tried interviewing her. She and her husband, or whoever he is... I've seen him wandering around Wildwood pretty late in the afternoon."

"What about Sampson Hawke?"

Jasmine shrugged. "I can't find any reason he would want Oliver out of the picture."

"But we still have the people that were on my list," said Barrett.

"I didn't get around to talking with Oliver's parents. I was kind of saving them for last. And Joe... Well, now you know the history of Joe. He wasn't a killer then, at the rest stop, and he isn't a killer now."

"Then we'll have to talk with Lyle and Sandra," said Barrett. "They're the only people who haven't been properly interviewed yet."

Jasmine checked the time. "Pineapple should still be open, right?"

Barrett nodded.

"Then let's go," Jasmine said.

"It's cold. It's rainy. And I have no idea where we are. Luffy, I think you've gone crazy."

Joe had been rambling thusly for the past twenty minutes. Talking softly to himself because, of course, it wasn't like the dog would understand him. But to his credit he was going along, braving the cold, wet weather.

Luffy still had no idea what he was looking for. Not consciously. But he had caught a scent, and it felt right. He was on his way. And every block they walked, the stronger the scene got. When it got weaker, he would double back and take a different course. By and by, he narrowed in on the source of the smell. And when he was almost close enough to taste it, he remembered what it was.

A strong whiff of perfume, which smelled the same as a vague hint he had caught wafting off Oliver Bridges that day in the dining hall, when he and Jasmine were talking over some philosophical mumbo jumbo.

They rounded the corner, and saw a tall, blonde woman walking briskly away from them. She was holding an umbrella, but a moment later she collapsed it and tucked it under her arm as she stepped off the sidewalk and approached the door of a small, ivy-covered townhouse.

"Whaddya know?" Luffy said, cocking his head. "If that isn't the place from Jasmine's vision, then I don't walk on four feet."

"This sucks," Joe grumbled quietly to himself.

"Don't worry," Luffy said. "You'll be able to tuck that cold hand of yours into your pocket. Let me just free it up."

He bolted forward, yanking the leash straight through Joe's cold, weak hand. It splashed down and dragged along the wet pavement behind Luffy as he sprinted down the sidewalk.

"Hey!" Joe yelled. "Luffy, come back! What's got into you?"

The blonde woman looked back just as she opened the door. Her eyes widened with fear as she saw Luffy. She stepped into the house quickly and slammed the door shut, yelling something about a rapid dog in the neighborhood. Or maybe it was rabid; that was far meaner and less accurate.

"Crap," Luffy said. He looked back and saw Joe closing in, a skeletal man in dirty clothes.

"I hate to do this to you, buddy," Luffy said. "But I've gotta run again."

He turned right and dodged Joe's swinging arms, running into the narrow alley that led along the outside of the townhouse. Joe could have fit, but he didn't dare follow. There were too many windows, too many chances to be spotted and labeled a peeping tom.

"I'll be right back!" Luffy called.

He slowed down as he approached the back corner and hunkered down in the gravel, behind a waterlogged bush. Ignoring Joe's harsh whispers, he turned his attention toward what was happening in the back yard.

There was the sound of a patio door sliding open, and voices caught in the middle of conversation.

"-don't really see what the big deal is," a familiar voice said.

"Care to share with the class?" Luffy asked, smiling as he panted in the clammy air.

Sampson Hawke and the blonde woman stepped into his view, carrying glasses of wine out to sit under an awning. Under the gloomy, muffled glow of a single porch light they sat and shared a quick toast.

"There's plenty to worry about, Sampson," the woman said.

"Why? Did Lyle find out?"

"As far as I know, he might have," said the woman.

"Sandra, slow down. Tell me what's going on."

Sandra. Where had Luffy heard that name before?

"Okay," Sandra said with a long sigh. She took a drink of wine that was even longer, draining half the glass. "I don't know when it happened, but my ring is gone. I haven't been able to find it. As far as I know I left it at home in my bedside table the last time we met."

"But it isn't there?" Sampson asked.

She gave him a look. And if looks could kill, Sampson Hawke would have been dead.

"No, darling," she said sarcastically. "It isn't. If it was, we wouldn't have a problem."

Sampson looked scared. "You don't think Oliver would have told him, do you?"

Sandra shook her head as she took another swallow of wine. "Oliver was sworn to silence. He would have held his knowledge of our affair over my head for the rest of his life, using it to get his way. He wouldn't have given that power up for anything. And now he has no power at all."

Her voice was flat, devoid of any kind of emotion.

"Then how could Lyle have found out?" the professor asked.

"He's not an idiot, Sampson. Far from it. He could have sussed it out in any number of ways. There's no love lost between Lyle and me. Our marriage is nothing more than a symbol at this point. And I'm fine with that. Lyle's money and your attention. Life was perfect before my brat of a son found us out. But even now, I'm not going to give up what I have."

"Not even for love?" Sampson asked, pushing his glasses up.

She reached across to cup his cheek. "Not even for love. Darling, I don't think it's a good idea for us to see each other for a while. I came here to give you a warning. The ring disappeared before Oliver died. For all I know, he's the one who took it as part of some strange game. But just in case..."

"I'll watch myself," Sampson said. "You do the same."

"That's what I've been doing for twenty-three years," Sandra replied. "Lyle is a bastard. A brute. And he and I made a bastard, brutish son..."

She shifted in her chair, glancing back. She saw Luffy there and jumped up, nearly spilling her wine.

"There's that dog again!" she said.

Sampson narrowed his eyes. "Is that...?"

Luffy quickly retreated, backing down the narrow alleyway. He felt Joe grab him from behind, pulling him.

"Don't pull a stunt like that again!" the man said. "Jasmine asked me to take care of you, and that's what I'm going to do."

"Yeah, yeah, I hear ya," Luffy said. "Quick, we gotta get out of here!"

Joe didn't need any encouragement for that. He obviously felt ill at ease in such a well-to-do neighborhood, the windows of fancy houses staring at him like accusatory eyes. They took off running together, and didn't look back.

"I've dug up a big old bone this time!" Luffy said proudly. "Wait till Jasmine hears about this!"

Chapter 17

The restaurant Pineapple took up a whole block in downtown New Market. The building itself stood at the center, with parking lots and a literal park surrounding it, where people walked and enjoyed the air after their meals. As she and Barrett pulled up, Jasmine stared around with wide eyes.

"I kind of want to check out a menu just so I can see how expensive this place is," she said.

Barrett keyed the engine off. "My sister and her fiancé came here on Valentine's Day. They spent three hundred dollars between them without even trying. And they didn't even get dessert."

"Yikes," said Jasmine. "That's half of my month's rent."

Barrett pointed at the park area. "See those trees? They're not native to New York. They're not even native to America, I guess. They're some exotic thing from Africa or something like that. Lyle and Sandra had to get special permission from the governor to plant them here."

"Luffy would love to pee on those," Jasmine remarked. "You don't get a chance to mark your territory on an exotic tree that often. Maybe one day we'll travel somewhere faraway together..."

She leaned her head back and stared at the walkers wistfully, dreaming of another life where her bank account was always full and she could do what she wanted.

"Sorry about Luffy," Barrett said. "I know you wish he could be here right now. But maybe this is best. I don't think Lyle would be too happy about a dog coming into his restaurant."

"Yeah, you're probably right. But we can swing back around my apartment after this and see if they're back yet."

Barrett nodded. He pulled out a pad of paper and a pen, which he proceeded to click several times.

"You do the talking, and I take the notes," he said. "Sound good?"

"Peachy," Jasmine said. And she meant it.

Her bravery only lasted until she stepped out of the car and realized what she was wearing. The same lazy clothes she had slapped on after her run this morning. A highly mismatched set of dark jeans and a graphic tee shirt of a smiling avocado, which she usually used as pajamas. Then she looked around the parking lot and realized that every car here was foreign and very expensive.

"This is not where I belong," she said.

"Not yet," Barrett replied. "You've got a bright future ahead of you, Jasmine."

"Not this bright. Not with an English degree."

He shrugged. "I wouldn't be so sure. Just act natural. I've got my badge... that's all we need."

They approached the restaurant and entered the vestibule, where leather benches sat to either side. A few old ladies were waiting here, resting as their husbands paid the check on their lavish meal. Barrett nodded to them, trying clumsily to tip a nonexistent hat.

As they stepped through into the restaurant proper, Pineapple was revealed to them. It was all polished hardwood and crystal chandeliers, immaculate snow-white table cloths and spotless floors. The wait-staff was dressed to the nines in starched suits, not a single hair on their heads out of place. They moved to and fro with stunning grace, almost like they were dancing. Their legs seemed to move slowly even as they zoomed across the dining area, the trays in their hands never moving an inch.

"Whoa," Jasmine said.

"I know, right?" said Barrett.

She shook her head in disbelief. "I guess with a name like Pineapple I expected it to be a little tackier."

She nearly jumped in surprise as someone approached from her rear and laid a hand gently upon her shoulder. A man stepped into view, and there was no doubt at all, even if she hadn't seen the name tag, that this was Lyle Bridges. Even ignoring the resemblance to Oliver, there was an air about him. The air of a leader, a man who was confident and used to being in charge. Jasmine was instantly mesmerized by his easy charm and good looks, but she forced herself to remember the way he had treated Joe.

"It's a funny story, actually," he said, smiling between her and Barrett. "I had everything put together. I had furniture and decor ordered, staff interviewed and in training, a menu made up and all the food ready to be stocked... but I just couldn't think of a name. As I wallowed in frustration, I found myself at a birthday party for a young niece of mine, and she was having pineapple upside down cake. Voila."

He laughed, making a gesture in the air like a magician summoning something out of thin air.

"Officer Barrett," he said, "very nice to see you. And you, madam, you must be Jasmine Moore. I'm very surprised not to have seen you earlier. In fact, I'm surprised I haven't seen either of you."

"Well, there's a simple reason for that," said Barrett. "You didn't return any of my calls, and I didn't want to bother you at this... vulnerable time."

"Ah, yes," said Lyle, folding his hands in front of him. "Vulnerable, indeed. But I'm in my element now. When I'm here at work, I feel like I'm disconnected from everything that happens out there." He gestured vaguely toward the doors. "Working helped me a lot when my mother died. And when my brother passed as well. And now it's helping me still."

Jasmine expected a bit of the facade to slip away then, but it didn't happen. Lyle went on grinning.

"I'd show you to a seat," he said. "Best seat in the house, actually... but I assume you aren't here to enjoy the food."

"I couldn't afford it," Jasmine said, remembering the deal; her talking, Barrett taking notes. It was meant to be a light joke, but Lyle took it seriously.

"It's true that my restaurant is steeply priced," he said. "But for good reason. I offer only the finest ingredients, some of which you can't find anywhere else in the country. But we do have our more affordable menu items. Right now we're offering a wild mushroom risotto that runs only forty dollars a plate."

"Very generous," she said with a smile, despite the fact that forty dollars was the sum of her usual weekly grocery trip. "But I've already eaten. We were just here to follow up with you after the tragedy that's happened, Mr. Bridges. Do you think we could have a moment of your time?"

"And by a moment," he said, "you mean..."

"As long as it takes," Jasmine replied.

He smiled. "Well, if you insist..."

"I do insist."

He gestured for them to follow, and then he let them back into the kitchen. It was brightly lit and, despite the busy activity taking place, it was also very clean. However, it was incredibly hot. She saw a waitress dabbing a sweaty chef's face with a wash cloth. The smells, however, were incredible. Deep and rich, unlike anything Jasmine had experienced. The plates she saw were like little artworks, little masterpieces of color and texture. More like experiences than actual meals. Which was a good thing, because it would have taken five such plates to fill you up.

"Through here," Lyle said.

He led them past the kitchen and into an office that was, blessedly, air conditioned. He shut the door, pulled the shades down over the window, and turned around rubbing his hands together.

"Where do we begin?" he asked.

Barrett took a seat. Jasmine elected to remain standing. Lyle was already tall enough without letting him tower over her further. She knew he could bowl her over without effort in any conversation, talk her down to a whisper and defeat anything she tried to say.

"Is your wife around, Mr. Bridges?" she asked. "I hoped to talk to Sandra as well."

"You just missed her, actually," Lyle replied, leaning on the edge of the desk and getting uncomfortably close. "Sandra comes and goes. Some days she helps out, some days she just sits at the bar and entertains people. She used to be a full-time employee, but that hasn't been necessary for some time."

"So, she's at home?" Jasmine asked.

Lyle shrugged. "I imagine so. But who knows? She could have gone to a movie, or shopping. It's none of my business."

"But you're married," Jasmine said.

"Yes. We're married, not glued at the hip. We have our own lives. She could be at home, or she could be anywhere else. What does it matter to you?"

"Mr. Bridges," Barrett said.

"Shh, let the girl talk. Let her answer on her own." Lyle stared down at Jasmine with penetrating eyes. "I just want to know why you're so curious about Sandra."

She stared right back at him, aware that her heart was beating fast and he could probably see it in her neck.

"Mr. Bridges," she said, "you're aware that your son's death is being treated as a homicide."

He nodded. "I'm aware. And?"

"And in most murder cases, the perpetrator is someone the victim knew well."

"You're suggesting me or my wife might have killed Oliver?" he asked with plain offense.

"Do you want me to answer that truthfully, or treat you like a baby?" she asked, glaring up at him.

He stared angrily for a moment. Then, strangely, a little smile crept across his features.

"I like you," he said. "I like people who can just say what they mean. Most are too cowardly. Isn't that right, Officer Barrett?"

"Sure," he said, completely oblivious of the undertone as he scrawled his notes.

Lyle finally stepped around his desk and sat down, inviting Jasmine to do the same. She lowered herself onto an available chair and waited, for Lyle seemed to be preparing some kind of speech. He seemed like a man who could have memorized a speech and recited it with little preparation, but he was taking his time. Which to her meant he would speak more or less off the cuff, and perhaps therefore more honestly.

"I can't speak for my wife," he said, "but I most assuredly did not kill my son."

This seemed to be a place where most people would stop and wait for another question. But Lyle was smart. He knew exactly the line of inquiry that Jasmine would take, and knocked down her questions before she could even think to ask them.

"Oliver was everything I wished to leave behind," he said. "I knew from his youth that he wouldn't ever care to take over Pineapple for me, but I didn't care. I had and still have capable workers, men and women I respect, any one of whom could easily take control upon my retirement. I have a passion for food, but only because I have a passion for making people happy. One of the easiest ways to do that is through the taste buds.

"But my own son's happiness was important to me, as well. I let him follow his own path. Like me, he was always very smart. Very observant. But his passion led him to use his gifts differently. He was always introspective, looking at the way people think to see why they act the way they do. Figuring them out, empathizing with them. I dare say, and don't quote me on this, Oliver was the only person living or dead who ever truly loved my wife Sandra. He saw her evil and he accepted it. He sought to protect himself and his father from it, but he also tried to protect her.

"Not to say I'm not a bit evil myself," he added, fixing Jasmine with a meaningful gaze. Obviously he was referring to the incident with Joe. Somehow he knew the two of them were connected, but that was probably just owing to his position in the community. Jasmine doubted anything escaped him.

"But," he went on, "I know how to recognize the good in others. My son was good, and you shouldn't let any jealous, ignorant person tell you otherwise. Always he held in his heart the desire to improve the station of others. If I may make a rather bold comparison, I always likened him to the Buddha. A person who had it all but saw that others did not, and wanted to understand and ease their sorrows. He had no reason to care about anyone else, except that it was in his heart to do so. He wasn't much like his parents in any way. I accepted him, but Sandra did not. I think she hated him from the time he was an infant."

"Enough to kill him?" Jasmine asked.

He shrugged. "You might think I know my wife well after over two decades of marriage. But you might as well ask me to describe the inner feelings and features of a rock. The woman knows nothing other than the selfish pursuits of her desires and the fulfillment of her laziness. As long as you keep her happy, she's pleasant enough to be around. And I have mastered the art of keeping her happy. But..."

Lyle's confidence finally showed a few cracks. His eyes darted away from Jasmine's for just a moment. When they came back, they burned with a weaker light than before.

"But," he went on, "for a week or two leading up to Oliver's death, she was in a sour mood. Nothing could make her happy. She was short with me and the staff, and I eventually ordered her to stay home. She was insufferable. I can't say I know for certain what was the matter. But I can say that she's been more or less back to her old self ever since Oliver left us."

He looked down at his desk, idly touching the edge of a picture frame. Jasmine couldn't see the picture itself from where she was sitting, but she would bet her life that it was a photo of Oliver.

"Has she shown any remorse at all?" Jasmine asked.

"Sure, a little. The bare minimum to be expected from a grieving mother. I'm not one to call out sexism against my own privileged gender, but I feel like mothers get a free pass when a child dies that is rarely awarded to fathers. They are allowed to grieve in their own way, at their own time. It isn't seen as strange or suspicious that Sandra hasn't been crying.

But everyone I've come across since my boy died seems to think there's something wrong with me, that I'm still working, still doing the things that keep me sane."

He shrugged.

"Sandra is an actress at heart," he said. "She pretended to love me, and I fell for it. She pretended to want to marry and have a child, and I fell for that as well. After that, when she knew she was anchored to me, she stopped pretending. She showed her true reptilian self. But now that Oliver is gone, she's pretending again. She knows how to use her crocodile tears. I don't know the true Sandra. She probably doesn't even know herself. Maybe there's nothing there at all... just a blank shell full of nothing but the base needs of a human being. Food, water, air, distraction. Do I think she could have killed my son? Yes. Do I think she actually did it? I don't know. I have no evidence to support it."

"Nothing?" Jasmine asked.

He shook his head. "Sorry."

"Do you think she could have done it to spite you?"

He laughed at that. "To spite me? The prerequisite of that is she would have to hate me first. But for her to truly hate me, she would have had to care about me in any way at one point or another. If she did do it, it wasn't to get back at me. That's for sure. She doesn't care. I'm sure I rarely enter her thoughts at all."

There was silence for a moment, filled only by the soft noise of Barrett's pen gliding over paper.

"To coincide with Sandra's change in demeanor," Lyle went on, "Oliver went through his own change, in the days leading to his death."

"What sort of change?" asked Jasmine.

"He seemed... avoidant. He didn't speak to me as often. We rarely saw him except here at Pineapple, which I suppose he saw as safe harbor. Enough witnesses and bystanders that nothing could happen."

"What was he worried about? What did he think could have happened?"

"I really don't know. Another blowup between Sandra and me, maybe. I've made my peace with who I'm married to a long time ago, but she is truly a spoiled brat. If she doesn't get what she wants from me, presents and all that, she'll get nastier and nastier until I relent. It causes fights now and then."

"If I could butt in really quick," Barrett said, "it sounds like you hate this woman. Why not get a divorce?"

"Because by law she owns half of everything," Lyle said. "I might as well kiss Pineapple goodbye, even though I'm the one who created it, made it what it is... that's the legal system for you. Besides, I'm making it all out to be worse than it is. We fight now and then, but most of the time we get along. I guess it would be more accurate to say we coexist peacefully. She doesn't bother me, and I don't bother her."

Jasmine nodded. "But if she killed Oliver..."

Lyle frowned. "That would change everything. It would take a half dozen cops to keep me from my revenge. It would also mean I could divorce her without giving up anything but... I would trade it all to have my son back."

He frowned, sniffing once, and that seemed to be all the emotion he was prepared to display. Perhaps if he was at home, and not in this professional environment, he would have behaved more genuinely.

"Is there anything else?" he asked. "I'm afraid I can produce no damning evidence at the moment."

"There's one more thing," said Jasmine. She pulled the baggie of her backpack and showed it to Lyle. "Is this your wife's ring?"

He nodded with hesitation. "That's the one. Cost a fortune, but back then I thought she was worth it. I hadn't even noticed it was missing. How did you come across it?"

Jasmine looked at Barrett. The question now was, how much should they reveal to Lyle? There was no right or wrong answer, and Barrett nodded to show her it was up to her own discretion.

She turned the bag around. "Whose handwriting do you think this is?"

Lyle narrowed his eyes and sat forward to look more closely. But it didn't take him long to answer.

"It looks like Oliver's," he said. "I can't be sure, but it does look like it. Do you mind telling me what this is all about?"

He seemed to be sweating now. His heart must be racing. Thoughts must be whirling through his mind at a million miles per hour. But why not? What parent wouldn't be sweating, or experiencing palpitations when they were faced with these things?

"I can tell you," said Jasmine. "Professor Alan Keller claims someone left this ring and this note on his desk. I don't know how to figure out this mess I'm in. Hopefully someone will come along who does. Hold on to this for me. I can't trust anyone else right now. That's what the note says. Does it mean anything to you?"

Lyle shrugged. But it was not the casual, almost flippant shrug he would have given a few minutes ago. It was a heavy gesture, loaded with weight, and as his shoulders sunk the rest of him seemed to sink right along with them.

"It could mean any number of frightening things, couldn't it?" he asked. "But maybe it's safe to assume that the most likely and natural explanation is also the right one. Oliver felt he was trapped between Sandra and me. Trapped between love for his father and love for his mother. I think it was probably something like that. As for why he would take his mother's ring and give it over to someone... I don't really know."

Especially to someone who disliked him, Jasmine thought.

But then again, he might not have known that Keller disliked him. Maybe Oliver respected the professor quite a lot, trusted him more than anyone else... If he was as forgiving and caring as Lyle made him out to be, this seemed perfectly possible.

At any rate, it was almost sad to see the mighty Lyle Bridges in such a state. Collapsing in on himself, falling to pieces. It was like watching a strong, sturdy bridge, which you've driven across a hundred or a thousand times, suddenly being swallowed up and ripped to shreds by a flood. She decided now would be the time to leave.

"Thank you very much, Mr. Bridges," she said, standing up. "I appreciate the time you've given us. And I really mean that."

He smiled and nodded absently as she and Barrett made their way out.

"Do you think he'll be okay?" Barrett asked.

"That depends," said Jasmine. "If it turns out Sandra killed Oliver, I don't think he will be."

"But we have to be open to the possibility, right?"

She nodded. "The truth will win out, in the end."

Chapter 18

For the second time in recent memory, Jasmine found someone waiting outside her apartment door. This time it wasn't Joe. This time, it was someone whose face was wet not from sweat or from rain, but from tears.

"Alicia," Jasmine said, wrapping the girl in a hug. "I feel like I haven't seen you in forever. I was worried about you."

Alicia seemed oddly defensive, refusing to return the hug and even step away from her. From behind Jasmine, Officer Barrett cleared his throat awkwardly.

"Are you sure you want to do this?" he asked.

"Do what?" Jasmine asked.

His eyes flicked over to her. "I was asking her."

Jasmine turned her head, staring into her friend's eyes. Or trying to. Alicia could not meet her gaze.

"I'm sorry, Jasmine," she choked out through suppressed tears.

"For what?" Jasmine asked.

Alicia's chin trembled. "I was just walking around campus when a police car pulled up. They asked me if I could help them with something. They were asking a lot of people. But..."

"You were the one who identified that tag from my backpack," Jasmine said.

Alicia nodded. "I'm the reason you got arrested. I'm sorry, Jasmine. I'm so, so sorry."

"For what?" Jasmine asked with a smile. "For telling the truth? You didn't do anything wrong."

"Of course I did!" Alicia replied.

"But you didn't," said Jasmine. She turned away, leaning on the railing. She stared over the edge, out across the rain-soaked parking lot. "Actually, you helped me out. I'm starting to see something, now. I think I'm starting to figure something out... but it's too early to really tell."

Her heart was thumping. Her mind was racing as she tried to drag that creeping suspicion up to the front of her mind and shine an analytical light on it. Like a name or a word dancing on the tip of her tongue, she couldn't quite figure out what she was feeling. It was the most frustrating feeling in the world.

Suddenly, her thumping heart started to beat faster. Her vision narrowed in toward a point, and she felt a strange chill passing over her.

Another vision was coming.

Jasmine felt her legs going weak. She started to fall forward slowly, leaning out over the railing further and further like a drunk at a party. The last thing she saw before her eyes clouded over completely was the hard ground below. In another second, she was going to topple over into thin air.

Fear passed through her like an electric current. She caught her feet on the floor beneath her and jerked herself back. At the same time, she felt Barrett and Alicia both grabbing her from behind to help out. She stumbled backward a bit, knocking against a column. Her vision filtered back in, and her heart rate slowly returned to normal.

She hadn't seen anything. The vision had passed her by, offering none of its secrets.

If she had been alone, she would have cursed and punched the closest available surface. Potentially vital information had just flown straight past, irretrievable. What was she going to do now?

"Sorry about that," she made herself say. "I was just trying to get inside Oliver's head. What he must have been thinking right before he fell. I guess I started to slip, though. The railing's pretty slick."

They seemed to buy it, or else they decided it wasn't worth questioning her further.

She turned to Alicia. "As long as you're on the topic of telling the truth... do you think there's anything else you want to get off your chest? Anything you want to explain?"

Alicia took a deep breath. "I guess there could be a couple things."

Barrett gestured toward the apartment door. Jasmine took the spare key out of her bag and opened it up. They stepped inside, removing their wet shoes, and sat together in the tiny living room.

"Last time I was here," Alicia said, "I was in a dark place. Not as dark as the place I went to right afterward but... pretty dark."

"Did it have something to do with Oliver?" Jasmine asked.

Alicia laughed, wiping a tear from the corner of her eye. "It had everything to do with Oliver. Have you ever met my sister, Jasmine?"

"I've seen her a few times," Jasmine replied. "We don't have any of the same classes, obviously."

Alicia nodded. "She's beautiful, isn't she?"

"I guess so."

"She's prettier than I am."

"I don't know about that."

Alicia shrugged. "Well, I think most people think she is. Including Oliver. He was in love with my sister, Jasmine. He was too shy to ever show it around, but I found out. I caught him writing a love letter to her one day. Then I found a whole stash of them in Morgan's room. When she caught me looking at them, she laughed and told me all about how this weird, quiet kid at school had a crush on her. She thought it was all a big joke. And now I'm starting to see that it is, isn't it? A big old cruel cosmic joke! She had his love, and she treated it like garbage. And I was in love with Oliver... he was everything I ever wanted. But he barely knew I was there."

She shrugged, letting out a long sigh that stuck and shuddered in her chest for a moment.

"So," she went on, "that's what I was freaking out about that night, Jasmine. Me and Morgan were texting about Oliver. I was trying to convince her to help me out. I thought maybe if he couldn't have her, he could settle for me. It was stupid and I knew it, but I couldn't help but try. She just wouldn't help me out. She refused. She made fun of me..."

"I'm sorry, Alicia," Jasmine said.

"You've got nothing to be sorry about. I do. I've been a mess. Oliver and I never talked more than thirty seconds at a time, and here I am crying over him like he was my husband. Missing school, tanking my grades. God, I'm such an idiot."

"No you're not," Barrett suddenly interjected. "When I was your age, I got in a fight to try and win over a girl I liked. I got my butt kicked, and she still didn't like me afterward. That was stupid. You can't help the things you feel, Alicia. Feelings aren't really ours to control, even though we sometimes wish they were."

Jasmine looked back at the officer, giving him a nod. "I was trying to think of what to say, but I guess that does it."

He returned her nod. "I've got your back. Sometimes I arrest burglars. Sometimes I rescue ducklings from sewer drains. And sometimes I give love advice. It's all part of the job."

"Well, thanks, both of you," Alicia said. "I feel a lot better now, actually. I wish Oliver was still here, but..." She shrugged. "I don't have the power to bring him back. I'll just have to live with that. Along with what I did to you, Jasmine."

Jasmine scooted closer, giving her friend another hug. This time it was returned in earnest.

"How many times am I going to have to say it?" Jasmine said. "You didn't do anything wrong. I'm fine, I promise. And I don't care if I have to keep saying it forever, Alicia. I'm fine."

She nodded, sobbing in Jasmine's arm and soaking the shoulder of her shirt with tears.

There were noises outside the apartment door. Footsteps, and paw steps. Dog claws clicking on the balcony. The door opened; Joe and Luffy came in, both looking wet and quite haggard.

But the dog filled back up with energy as soon as he saw who was inside. He grinned from ear to ear and sprinted forward, leaping five horizontal feet to land like a crazy ball of fur straight in Jasmine's lap.

"You're alive!" he said.

"I was only in jail," she replied. "I wasn't dead."

"I heard dogs perceive time differently because they don't live as long," said Barrett. "To them it really does feel like we're gone forever when we go to the store or whatever."

"Thanks for reminding me of my mortality, officer," Luffy remarked. "Jasmine! You'll never guess what happened..."

He proceeded to explain it all to her. How he had taken Joe for a ride, the things he had seen and heard. Meanwhile, everyone else in the apartment engaged in an awkward chorus of hellos and how-are-yous. Joe looked like the most uncomfortable man in the world, and he kept glancing at Jasmine, begging with his eyes for her to rescue him. But she was too busy listening to the dog's story, a testimony that no one else could hear.

When Luffy was finished, Jasmine leaned her head back and tried to figure out two things at once. Her mind was split into two different trains of thought. One of them tried to discern what Luffy's observations meant. The other tried to determine how to broach it all with Barrett and the others without it seeming like she had plucked information out of thin air.

Maybe, she thought, she would keep them in the dark for now. She smiled as a plan came into her mind fully formed. A way forward, a way to wrap all of this up. Of course there was one crucial piece of information missing - the perpetrator. But she would just have to have faith in herself.

"Barrett," she said, finally breaking into the dying conversation. "I need to ask you another favor. You got me out of my classes at Wildwood for a week. Now I need you to get everyone else back at Wildwood."

He sat forward, nodding. "Just tell me when."

"No time like the present," she said.

He glanced at his watch. "It's almost nine o'clock, Jasmine."

"What's your point?" she asked. "We don't want to interrupt classes, do we? This seems like the perfect time."

Barrett shrugged. "If that's what you think is best. Who do we want to be there?"

"Let's see," Jasmine said. She pulled the old list out of her bag. The one Barrett had originally given her. She read the items out loud. "Lyle Bridges. Sandra Bridges. Joe Sanderson. Alan Keller."

Joe stepped forward, craning his neck to peer at the list.

"What is that?" he asked.

"A list of suspects," said Jasmine. "Don't worry. I think we can pretty much cross your name off."

She took out a pen, but she didn't cross any names off. Instead, she wrote in the number five beneath the last item on the list.

"Who else?" she asked. "Obviously we want Elden DuPont to be there."

She wrote in his name, then moved on.

"Charles Dane," Barrett suggested.

Jasmine nodded and added it in.

"Charles?" Alicia asked.

"We have our reasons," said Jasmine. "We can also add Sampson Hawke, for reasons that will become clear to you all soon. Then we can also add Lucille Whitaker and her husband."

"Why them?" Alicia asked.

"Just trust us," Barrett said with a smile. "Who else, Jasmine?"

"Obviously, you and I and Alicia will be there as witnesses," she said. She turned to her friend. "If you want to come, anyway."

Alicia nodded, giving the thumbs up.

"Anyone else?" asked Barrett.

Jasmine thought for a moment, then shook her head. "No. I think this is it." She tapped the list with her finger. "If someone did kill Oliver Bridges, their name is on this list."

"Hold on," said Luffy. "You didn't add me. Don't you think I could have killed him?"

Smiling, Jasmine leaned forward and scrawled one last name on the list. Everyone burst out laughing.

"This is ridiculous, isn't it?" Barrett asked.

"Yes," said Jasmine. "But it's kind of fun, too."

"Speak for yourselves," Joe said miserably.

Barrett stood up and gave the drifter a pat on the back. "Chin up, Joe. You're off the hook until Jasmine says differently. If you come through this clean, I'll see what I can do to get you some work around here."

Joe nodded, letting out his breath. "Okay. Let's do it."

Chapter 19

It wasn't easy as it seemed to get everyone gathered at Wildwood. They had to get Sandra's phone number off Lyle who they had trouble reaching due to a sudden late rush at Pineapple. However the restaurant closed at ten that night, and he promised he would be along with Sandra in short order.

Sampson Hawke proved equally tricky to wrangle in. He didn't answer his phone calls. Finally, Barrett had to look up his address and stop by his place to ask him to come to Wildwood. Jasmine, riding along in the passenger seat of the cruiser, was able to get a look at the house and confirm that it was the one from her vision.

As for visions... the one she had missed out on, the one she had skipped past, still haunted her. Perhaps if she had seen it, she would already know who had killed Oliver. But now she was on her own. Nothing but the regular, normal, non-psychic part of her mind to figure this puzzle out.

Sampson eyed her as he came down the front walk, unlocking his own car and climbing inside.

"He'll follow us to Wildwood," Barrett said as he got behind the wheel. "And I think that's everyone."

Jasmine nodded. It was 10:15 p.m.. The night was dark, but not so dark as it could have been. The crescent moon shone through, its glow reflecting and redoubling off the cloud cover. But a storm front seemed to be moving in fast. The thin, gray clouds began to muster their forces, gathering into dense, black thunderheads. Jasmine heard the first rumblings as they turned around and headed out of town, toward the college. As they zoomed along the deserted road, past hushed forests, the first raindrops began to fall. They splattered against the windshield in huge drops. Slowly at first, and then in stunning multitudes. Barrett switched on his high beams and slowed down, wary of every curve on the road. With a curtain of rain always a few feet ahead of them, it was difficult to see what was coming.

"Well, it's a good night for it anyway," he said with a smile. "Dark and stormy."

Jasmine twisted around, staring out through the rain-blurred back window at the set of headlights behind them. Sampson was still following them. A display of innocence? If he was guilty and scared, she thought he might have peeled off and skipped town. But if he was guilty and confident... why not play along? He would know there was no real evidence, or else he would have been arrested rather than asked along to some late-night game of charades.

Jasmine smiled, petting Luffy where he lay in the backseat. Getting a good nap in after the events of the day. He snored almost loud enough to drown out the rain.

"Here we are," Barrett said.

Wildwood appeared around the corner. Only the bare minimum of lights were on, lighting the grounds in little pools of yellow light that stood few and far between. The entire building and especially the clock tower loomed against the stormy sky, shadowed and silent.

But Wildwood was not abandoned, not even at this late hour. There were five cars already parked in the same lot, separated by empty spaces. Just off the parking lot, up a narrow pathway, a sheltered doorway stood open and waiting, letting out a pool of light upon the wet pavement.

Barrett pulled into an empty spot and put the car into park. They waited as Sampson Hawke parked his own car and got out, staring at them through the rain with a look of annoyed expectance.

Jasmine got out first, opening the back for Luffy. He climbed out clumsily, pausing with only his front paws on the pavement to stretch. His eyes were still half closed, blinking every time a drop of rain hit them.

"Are we there yet?" he asked.

"We're here," Jasmine said. She looked at Barrett. "Whatever happens, I have a feeling this is going to be the end. Do you trust me?"

He nodded. "Obviously."

Standing a few yards away, Sampson impatiently tapped his watch.

"I have a bed time, you know," he said.

"Hold your horses, old man," Luffy barked.

Obviously Sampson did not understand the words, but he still took a startled step back. Clearly his conscience was guilty about the affair at least, and what Luffy had seen. He looked at Jasmine with fear in his eyes for a moment. Perhaps he was wondering how much she knew. After all, Luffy could not have been out there at his house alone.

Barrett led the way inside. They walked down a side hallway and entered the music room. Everything but the chairs had been moved aside; everyone else was already gathered and waiting.

Charles Dane had abandoned his chair in favor of restless pacing. Lyle Bridges stood alone, sipping from a metal flask in the shadows of the corner. His wife was chatting animatedly with Alicia, who looked quite disquieted and uncomfortable. Joe sat somewhat near to her, looking like he wanted to help but not daring to try for fear of the wicked woman.

The Whitakers, sans their young child, sat close together and held hands, looking perhaps like the most nervous of the bunch. They were all jumping legs and chewed lips.

Professor Keller alone seemed perfectly disinterested in what was going on. He had even brought a book, and was seated on the floor with his back against the wall, reading it.

Dean DuPont look angrier than anything. He stood in the middle of the room, ranting about how they were all being abused and manipulated. No one seemed to be listening to him very closely, but he had still taken on the galvanized conviction of a successful leader. He whipped around to face Jasmine and Barrett as they entered.

"Sampson," he said. "I see they've dragged you here too."

"Can it, DuPont," Barrett said. "You didn't have to come unless you wanted to."

"You really think I had a choice?" DuPont asked. "Did you think I was going to let a gathering like this happen at my college without me being present?"

"I was kind of hoping you might, yeah," Barrett replied.

DuPont frowned. "You're angry with me, Luke. Ever since I turned down your application to attend Wildwood, you've blamed me for everything."

"No, I just don't like you very much. There's a difference. I'm happy with my career."

DuPont made a face like a duck and turned away.

"Alright," Barrett called out across the room. "Everyone pay attention now. Jasmine, you have the floor."

She nodded, watching nervously as all eyes turned toward her. Barrett dragged a chair closer to the center of the room and sat down. Sampson remained standing and moved over near Keller, his arms folded.

"I called you all here to set a few things straight," Jasmine announced. "And hopefully to get to the bottom of what happened to Oliver Bridges."

A few wary glances passed around the room. Jasmine took note of them.

"First off, I want to say that this meeting has no time limit," she said. "I've asked Officer Barrett to keep you all here until I'm satisfied. It could be ten minutes, or two hours. It all depends."

"On what?" Sampson demanded.

"On how much I can learn," said Jasmine.

Sandra Bridges sneered. "Who died and made you Inspector?"

"A guy named Jack Torres," Jasmine replied. "Thanks for asking. The local police have asked me to help out, and I'm taking that job seriously."

"It's true," Lyle added. "She's taking it very seriously indeed. The girl has nerves of steel, so I wouldn't mess with her if I were any of you." He laughed and went on sipping at his flask. To him, this seemed like the entertainment of the century.

"So," Keller said, bookmarking his page and placing the book in his lap. "Where do we begin?"

Chapter 20

"First I need to identify someone," Jasmine said, pointing at Lucille's husband.

"Me?" he asked.

Jasmine nodded.

"She means she needs to know your name and who you are," said Lyle.

"Uh... well, I'm Marshall. Marshall Whitaker. Lucille is my wife."

"Marshall. Good to meet you. I'm Jasmine Moore."

"The sleuth," he said with a nod, his eyes shifting nervously to another member of the gathering.

Jasmine nodded. "I wanted to ask you something. And you, Lucille. I've often seen Marshall walking around at Wildwood late in the afternoon..."

Marshall smiled. "That's easy to explain. I've been picking up Lucille from work every day. I come to Wildwood when I get out and wait for her to finish. I feel weird about being in the buildings, so I usually walk around outside."

"Lucille, don't you have a car of your own?" Jasmine asked. "I remember I used to see your driving."

Lucille nodded. "I had a car of my own. Some thug decided to slash my tires. We've been saving up for the baby, so we haven't gotten new tires yet."

"That's right," said Marshall. "It's easy enough for me to just come pick her up. I work in the city, and it's on my way home."

"Okay. That makes sense. What's the latest you would say you've been at Wildwood, Mr. Whitaker?"

Marshall shrugged. "I don't know. Six. Seven, maybe."

"Thank you. That's all I need for now." Jasmine turned to the left. "Charles, I need to hear something from you now."

He stopped pacing and stared at her expectantly. He didn't look angry or worried. He just looked tired and vaguely bored, now.

"Go ahead," he said. "I have all night. Nothing waiting for me at home but an energy drink and a load of homework."

Jasmine once again brought out the bag containing the ring. Lyle let out a laugh and Sandra abruptly stopped talking. She was unable to suppress the gasp that came rushing out of her mouth.

"Do you recognize this?" Jasmine asked.

Charles stared for a moment in utter confusion. "I suppose I do after all. I remember now. It was sitting on Professor Keller's desk one day. I'm sure it's the same one."

"It is," Keller called from across the room.

"It came with a note," Jasmine said. "A note from Oliver Bridges. The ring might have contained some sort of evidence. But that was all ruined when you, Charles, started messing with it."

He shrugged. "It's just a ring. Besides, it was left before Oliver died. What sort of evidence could it possibly hold?"

"The identity of the wearer, perhaps," said Jasmine.

At that, Sandra relaxed. It was subtle. You would only notice if you were explicitly watching for it.

Charles shrugged again.

"I just want to know," Jasmine said, "why you felt the need to touch it?"

"Care to share with the class?" Sampson asked, his arms still folded. Sandra shot him a look, but it seemed the man couldn't help himself.

"If you all insist that I do so," said Charles. He stood up straight, clenching his jaw. "Alright, I'll say it. Perhaps I have been looking for a gift for a certain someone. Perhaps even unconsciously I have been looking for this gift, so that when I saw a pretty ring all alone without an obvious owner my fingers decided of their own accord to start toying with it. Perhaps, when I realized what I was doing and that such a ring couldn't possibly not have an owner when found in that context, I took my hands away."

He turned to face the room, and went on.

"There is a girl at Wildwood College whom I adore," he said. "She is known to you, Alicia. As you understand from the favor I asked of you. I do not care to reveal her identity at this moment. But I'm guilty only of the crime of love."

"And being a complete jerkwad," Luffy put in.

But Jasmine felt herself melting, some inner part of her going soft.

Alicia nodded along with all of this. The rest of the room was soon nodding as well.

"I didn't kill Oliver," Charles said. "It was true that I was angry at him, but I was angrier at myself for putting all of my eggs in one basket. Besides, anger is a far cry from hatred. And, seeing as I am not a psychopath, true hatred is the only thing that could ever motivate me to kill. Or self-defense, I suppose."

"Maybe Oliver attacked you," Sampson proposed.

"Don't be ridiculous," Lyle Bridges replied. "My son wouldn't attack anyone."

"But maybe," Jasmine said, turning to Oliver's father, "you didn't know your son in the same way as some people here. Professor Keller, isn't it true that Oliver was an annoyance in your class? That he would often talk over you and correct your statements?"

Keller nodded slowly. For the first time, he looked to be invested in this meeting.

"If he corrected this man," Lyle said, "it was because the professor got something wrong. My Oliver was passionate about knowledge, and the thought of letting any mistake slip past and root itself in the minds of his fellow students would have been akin to you, Jasmine, watching someone kick that dog of yours in the ribs and doing nothing about it."

Luffy barked. Jasmine winced at the thought.

"I don't doubt that about Oliver," she said. "But his passion for knowledge could have been misinterpreted. It could have festered as anger and then as hatred which, as Charles said, is a pretty good precursor to murder. So, what do you say, Professor Keller?"

"Did I kill Oliver?" he asked. "The thought is too crazy to entertain. I didn't like the kid, but my plan was just to bide my time until he was out of my class. Nothing more."

"Forgive me, Jasmine," Charles said, "but isn't this pointless? It's all he said, she said. Obviously no one's going to come out and say they killed the sod."

Jasmine nodded. "No. You're right. And I didn't think they would. But this whole time, I've been watching. I've been reading between the lines."

"Oh, here we go," Luffy said excitedly. "You're all in deep trouble, now."

"There's something going on here that I was confused about for the longest time," Jasmine went on. "But I think I'm starting to see it. The way I understand it now, there were three people somehow involved in Oliver's death."

"Wait, what?" Sampson demanded, stepping forward. "You can't just come out and say that! Where's your proof?"

"Hopefully, I won't need any proof," Jasmine replied. "Because I don't have any."

There were several other gasps. Lyle paused mid drink and stared at her.

"Like I said," she went on. "Three people were involved, but only one person actually killed him. That's the way I see it."

"Then what did the other two do?" Charles asked. "Tie the boy's shoelaces together so he was easier to trip?"

"Watch your mouth," Lyle snapped. "This isn't a joke."

"It seemed like a big joke to you a minute ago," said Charles. "Maybe you killed him."

"He didn't," Jasmine said. "At least, I don't think he did."

She felt a gentle touch on her elbow from behind, followed by quiet words from Barrett.

"I don't mean to interrupt," he said. "But we're going to need a stronger case than that."

"I'm working on it," Jasmine whispered back.

"Who were the three people?" Sandra asked.

"I only know two of them," said Jasmine. "They didn't help kill Oliver. They weren't accomplices. But they were witnesses. And for some reason they haven't come forward."

Everyone started looking around at each other, eyes wide with suspicion and fear.

"Who?" Charles asked.

"Lucille and Marshall," Jasmine said, pointing at them. "You two saw something. Didn't you?"

The husband and wife looked at each other. They looked like two people who were drowning, sharing one last moment of love before they sank down into the deeps and drifted away.

"But I won't press too hard on that right now," Jasmine added, throwing them a life preserver. "Actually, I want to talk more about this ring."

She opened the bag and dumped the piece of jewelry in question into her palm. Holding it out, she ambled around the room for a moment, looking at everyone, hold the ring up to their hands. The men smiled nervously, and Alicia and Lucille's eyes sparkled as they imagined such a ring belonging to them.

Finally, Jasmine came to Sandra Bridges. She grabbed the woman's hand and slid the ring onto the appropriate finger. The band and the gem perfectly covered a pale spot on the naked digit.

"It's your ring," Jasmine said.

"Well, I could have told you that," Sandra replied in a huff. "What a detective you are. My son must have taken it from me to use as collateral. He was always playing games, trying to use me for things..."

"No, he wasn't," Jasmine replied. "Your son wanted no drama. He loved you, and all he wanted was a normal life. But you're a miserable, terrible wife and a worse mother."

Sandra stared as though she had been slapped. Evidently she was not used to being talked to like that at all. She was stunned, forgetting even to be angry.

"Oliver had his reasons for what he did with the ring," Jasmine said. "I don't understand fully what they were. But I do know something that two people in this room have tried really hard to keep them hidden. A secret."

For a moment all was silent. You could have heard a pin drop. But instead, Jasmine heard a metallic clink as Lyle finally capped his flask and slipped it into his pocket.

"Mr. Bridges," Jasmine said. "Did you know Sandra was having an affair?"

He shrugged, seemingly unperturbed. "I generally assume she's having an affair at all times."

"But you didn't know for sure?"

He shook his head. "No."

"And you had no idea who she might be having an affair with?"

He shook his head again. Across the room, Sampson suddenly coughed a couple of times and crouched down to tighten the laces on his shoe.

"Do either of you want to admit what you've been doing?" said Jasmine.

"I don't know what you're talking about," Sandra spat. "You're a nosy little fool and I think DuPont should run you out of here, if he has any backbone at all."

"I won't be dictated to in my school!" DuPont shouted. "Just because your husband owns Pineapple-"

"I own Pineapple as well," Sandra replied. "Lyle and I are married."

"Maybe not for long," Lyle said quietly. "Go ahead, Jasmine. Don't let these morons get you off track. Tell us."

She nodded and all eyes were back on her, though some of them clearly wished to be looking at something else. A beach, or the bottom of a glass. Anything but her.

"Sampson Hawke and Sandra Bridges were having an affair," she said. "I don't know how long it's been going on, but Oliver knew about it. And I think it's possible that one of them killed him to keep the secret hidden."

Sampson looked startled at first, and then fully outraged.

"You think I could have killed Oliver?" he barked. "I had nothing to lose by him knowing about Sandra and I!"

"So you admit it," Lyle said.

"Yes, I admit it. I do, alright? It's been going on for six months."

"Seven," Sandra hissed.

"Whatever."

"So, I see how much I mean to you," she said, turning her head away from him. "You forget how long we've been seeing each other, and you throw me under the bus. You try and have me blamed for killing my own son."

"Well, it would have to be you!" Sampson said, stepping forward. "Jasmine, you must understand. You're smart. I'm sure you know what's going on. If Lyle ever found out about us, he would have asked for a divorce."

"We don't know that," Sandra said, rubbing the back of her neck.

"And her whole lavish lifestyle," Sampson went on, "her credit cards and all that, it would be gone. Sure, she'd get half of Lyle's assets. Maybe, if the court was unfair. But it probably wouldn't be that unfair, considering the conditions of adultery. But even if she got those assets, she'd squander them on plastic surgery and clothes in a week!"

"I can't believe you," Sandra said. "I really can't. To think I fell in love with such a weak, hateful man. It makes me sick at myself."

"You should be sick," said Lyle, stepping out of the shadows at last. "Everything about you is wretched and rotten. I wish I could go back in time and never marry you."

"Oh, yes, a fine idea," said Sandra, laughing and glancing around to see if anyone was laughing with her. "Then you would never had had a son."

"I might as well never have had him anyway," Lyle said. He sounded like he was choking on his own words. "He's gone now. Because of you."

"I didn't kill him," said Sandra. "No matter how mean of a person you think I am, do you really believe I could do that?"

"It's not a matter of belief," said Lyle. "Two months ago, my son came to me. It was late at night, at the restaurant. He told me something... he told me that he was worried about you and me, Sandra. About his parents. He said it was all a big tangled knot and he had been trying to figure out how to untie it ever since he could remember. But he couldn't figure it out, and now it was worse than ever. He said he was worried about you, and the things you might do. I know why he took the ring. He wanted help, and he wanted insurance against you. He wanted to make sure you would be held accountable for something for once in your life. That's why he did it!"

Sandra stared at the floor, shaking her head from side to side.

"I didn't!" she said. "I didn't do it!"

Lyle grabbed her by the arms. But rather than yanking her, he pulled her gently to her feet and spoke softly.

"You can stop lying now. Stop lying to me, and stop lying to yourself. It's all over. You have no choice. Jasmine, tell her."

"Actually," Jasmine said, "I don't know if it's that simple."

He looked at her, his mouth hanging open.

"We know Oliver was murdered," Jasmine went on. "And if that's the case, there's only one person who could have done it. I've heard everything. I've tried to puzzle out of everything in my head. And now I know who the killer is."

She turned in a slow circle, staring at each person in return. Only one person failed to meet her eyes.

"Barrett," she said. "Go stand over by the door. I don't want anyone getting out."

Barrett nodded and moved to do as she asked. His back was still turned, and he was only halfway to the door, when Elden DuPont suddenly burst forward. The officer turned around, reaching for his sidearm, just in time to be bowled over by the much larger man.

Barrett went down on his back, the wind crushed out of him. He grunted in pain and flipped over onto his belly, yanking his sidearm out of its holster and aiming it.

"Freeze!" he yelled.

But DuPont kept going. He threw his bulk against the door and fell through, his fancy shoes skidding on the floor. He nearly tore the door from its hinges in his haste to slam it shut... but it was stopped short by the outthrust arm of Charles Dane, who caught it and pushed it open again.

"After him!" Lyle shouted.

Jasmine was the second one to the door. She and Luffy ran through, turning just in time to see DuPont vanishing around a corner, headed deeper into the school.

"Luffy, you know what to do," Jasmine said.

"He's already in the bag," the dog said. He took off, moving as fast as his four legs could carry him.

Jasmine almost shouted instructions after him. What to do, and where to go. But there was no need. She already knew where this was going. Where it would end. It was fated.

Barrett and Charles piled into the hall after her, followed by Lyle Bridges.

"What do we do?" Lyle asked.

"We still have witnesses in the music room," said Jasmine. "Do you think you can keep everyone inside?"

Lyle nodded. "Count on it."

"Thanks. Charles, Luke, you're with me. Come on!"

She started running. For a moment she flashed back to a dark beach, another pursuit months in the past. She had been out of breath for ten minutes after that. She was glad she had started working out.

"What's the plan?" Barrett huffed out as he raced to keep up with her.

"There are only two places he can go," Jasmine said. "The road, or the woods."

"Well, he's gotta go towards the road! That's where his car is. That's his best bet for getting away."

"Then we'll cut him off," Jasmine said.

They took a short cut, following the same way they had used to come inside. In a moment they were outside, running along the edge of the parking lot in pounding rain. Jasmine was soaked to the bone in three seconds, splashing through puddles and squelching grass. The night was now as dark as a crypt, deep shadows obscured further by the rain. Only during the brief, distant flashes of lightning was it possible to see anything.

Jasmine stopped and turned around. "Charles, how many exits are there?"

"Why are you asking me?"

"Because you know the place the best out of the three of us. Come on! How many exits?"

"Um... four. The main doors. The side door we just came out of. And two other side doors."

"He's in a panic," Barrett said. "He'll go for the most obvious course. Like a scared animal. The front door."

"Are you sure?" Jasmine asked.

"As sure as I can be."

"Good enough for me," said Jasmine.

She led the way along the edge of the building, glancing in each window as she passed. But she could see nothing in any of them but her own reflection, sometimes thrown back at her as lightning burst toward the horizon.

As they neared the corner that would bring them in view of the front door, they heard distant barking.

"Luffy!" Jasmine cried.

She raced around the corner and saw the dog standing there in the rain, looking confused.

"I had him, Jasmine," he said. "But he must have given me the slip."

"Did he make it outside?" Jasmine asked quietly, crouching down to hug him.

"No, I don't think so. I think he's still in the building."

Jasmine stood and turned to the others. "I know exactly where he went."

Chapter 21

There were only two ways of reaching the top of the clock tower. An interior staircase, and a maintenance ladder outside. It was clear which way DuPont would have taken.

Jasmine sprinted through the dark main hall, nearly slipping several times in the water that was pouring off her. Luffy stuck by her side; Charles and Barrett trailed a little ways behind, breathing heavily in the quiet of the empty school.

Jasmine had only been in the clock tower once, but she remembered the way. In a moment she was racing up the steps two at a time, moving past old windows with yellow glass. She could sense DuPont up ahead, scared and confused, uncertain.

It seemed she had been running up those steps forever. Like this was all one big, extended vision, and it wasn't actually happening. Like she would never reach the top. But just when her legs were really starting to burn, the stairs ended in a small brick room. Dead ahead, standing wide open, was the door onto the balcony from which Oliver Bridges had fallen to his death. The wind drove rain in through the door. She ran down the steps in tiny, cold trickles.

Jasmine took a deep breath.

"I've got your back," Luffy said.

She strode forward, out onto the balcony, and saw DuPont immediately.

He was standing there with his hand on the support column, staring at the temporary chains and warning tape that had been struck up where Oliver had fallen through. He wasn't moving. He wasn't even trembling with cold or fear. He was like a statue.

"Dean DuPont," Jasmine said.

He glanced over at her, his eyes red and swollen with tears. "Yes, Miss Moore?"

"Care to take a step back?" she asked, offering him a smile.

"Maybe. Maybe not. I think I'll just stand here for a minute until I can decide."

"Officer Barrett is right behind me," Jasmine said. "He isn't going to let you do anything hasty."

DuPont smiled. "Just like he wasn't going to let me out of the music room. Luke was never very good at anything, except at having a heart... something I seem to struggle with."

"You can talk to me," Jasmine said. "I'm not just here to solve crimes. I'm here to learn. And to listen."

"Well, you won't be learning from me. Not anymore."

"Just tell me what happened, and we can figure out what comes next together," said Jasmine.

By now Charles and Barrett were at her back, waiting. Listening. Barrett had handcuffs ready. Apparently he had realized he didn't need his sidearm; it was back in its holster.

"It was never meant to happen," said DuPont, shaking his head.

"I'm sure it wasn't," said Jasmine. "But it did. And now it's time to share. You don't need to keep holding onto it anymore."

DuPont nodded. "It shouldn't have ever gone so far. He was standing here, right here, when I came up. He had asked me to meet with him. It was the evening, late, and I thought we were alone..."

"What did he say?" asked Jasmine.

"He pointed," said DuPont. "He showed me the crumbling cement. I knew about it, of course, but I had no idea it was so bad. He told me someone could die up here... I laughed and told him he was exaggerating." As an example, DuPont let out a dry, almost corpse-like laugh. "And then he began to threaten me. He told me as long as this was fixed, and he had his wishes for assigned parking and all those other items he was so set on, he would forget that I had let such an obvious violation sit unrepaired for so long. He wouldn't bring it up with the board, and I wouldn't get in trouble."

"Did you push him then?" asked Jasmine.

"No, not then," said DuPont. "Not before Oliver tried to frighten me. He stepped up on the rail, placing his feet between the uprights and his hands on the top. He started bouncing around, making the thing move. But it clearly didn't move as much as he thought it would. It flexed a little, but it was in no danger of ripping free. Or so it seemed. I was angry... very, very angry. I wasn't thinking clearly. All I wanted was to further call his bluff and weaken his position. So I gave him and the whole railing a push. He had tried to scare me, so I was going to do the same. I didn't expect the thing to... I didn't expect it..."

"It tore out of the concrete and fell," said Jasmine. "With Oliver still holding onto it."

DuPont let his head drop. "He tried to grab onto anything he could get. He had a handful of my coat for a second, but he slipped free. I must admit I was in too great of a shock to reach out and help him. I didn't think of it, until it was too late... and then I was just reaching into empty air. I swear it was never meant to be..."

"It was a terrible accident," said Jasmine. "You didn't murder Oliver Bridges, but you did kill him."

"Yes. I did. I admit my guilt. My career is over, and so is the college."

Barrett stepped forward now, raising his hands. The handcuffs were back on his belt.

"The college will be fine, as long as you don't jump," he said. "What you've just told us is a good start, Elden, but it's a far cry from a court testimony. If you go to trial and explain this in front of a judge, it'll be obvious that the school wasn't at fault. It was just you. The railing wouldn't have broken if you hadn't shoved it."

"And nothing will happen?" DuPont asked.

"Not to Wildwood, no. The school's reputation won't be tarnished. The railing will be repaired and that'll be that. You'll take the fall for everything."

DuPont took a deep breath, staring out into space. Finally he pushed off the column and turned to face justice.

"I'll go with you," he said. "For the greater good."

Chapter 22

"We didn't see the whole thing," Lucille said, cradling her child to her chest. "But we heard it. A cracking, grinding sound. A scream. A horrible, horrible scream... And then we saw Oliver lying there on the ground. And up at the top, standing there in the open with his hands sticking out..."

"Elden DuPont," Barrett said.

Marshall nodded. "We tried to get away. He caught up to us on the road and cut us off. Nearly drove us into the ditch. I've never seen someone act so crazy. He had a baseball bat, and he threatened us. He threatened my wife and my unborn daughter. If we told anyone, he would ruin us."

"Were those his exact words?" Jasmine asked.

Marshall cringed. "No. Not his exact words. The words he used were more... graphic."

"So, you bought into his threat," Jasmine said.

"How could we not?" said Marshall. "It's different when you're alone, or even when you're just with another adult. But when you have kids... especially when one of them is still in the womb..."

Jasmine nodded, looking at Lucille. "So that was the reason you were so rude when I interviewed you."

"Sorry," said Lucille, wincing. "I was scared, Jasmine. I just wanted to get rid of you."

"I understand. And so does Barrett. Right?"

Barrett nodded. "All's well that ends well. No reason to drag anyone else through the mud. We have a full confession from DuPont. He's pleading guilty. He wants to go away. There's no reason to even bring your eyewitness account into it."

"Unless we have to," Marshall said.

"We won't," said Barrett. "That's a promise. If you think it would help clear your conscience, you're welcome to testify anyway."

The married couple shared a long look that was quite meaningful, but whose meaning was lost on Jasmine.

"Maybe," said Lucille. "We'll think about it."

The Whitakers left soon thereafter. Jasmine, Luffy and Barrett were alone in the interview room at last. All was silent for a moment.

"Well," said Jasmine.

"Yup," Barrett replied.

"I guess that's another case down," said Jasmine. "I kind of thought I'd never figure this one out."

"But you did, in the end," said Barrett.

"Actually I didn't."

The cop stared at her. "Huh?"

Luffy stared too. "What?"

Jasmine shrugged. "I had it narrowed down to Sandra or DuPont. I was trying to get one of them to finally crack up. And it worked."

"Well, that's a legendary move," Barrett said.

"It was nothing," Jasmine replied.

"Why were you so sure it was one of those two, though?'

"Well... Sandra was obvious. The woman is a snake. But DuPont was looking shifty the whole time. And besides I had already directed my questions at everyone else in the room by the time Lyle and Sandra got into their shouting match. They all seemed rock solid. But I hadn't spoken to DuPont yet."

"So it had to be him."

"It stood to reason, yeah."

Barrett laughed. "Has anyone ever told you that you'd be a great cop?"

"I may have heard it once or twice," Jasmine replied.

"Then I'll try not to sound like a broken record. But I have a couple other things I've been wondering about. I don't know if I'll be able to sleep until I know the answers."

"Then ask."

"Okay. There's Oliver, right? Nice kid. Selfless. So, why did he act that way with DuPont? Why start throwing out threats?"

"I was wondering that too," said Jasmine. "But I think the answer is pretty simple. He was guilty. He was ashamed. Because he knew what his mom was doing, and he was trying to figure out what to do about it. So he was flailing, and he latched onto the only thing he had any power in. He tried to keep his head above water by dunking DuPont's head under."

"Couldn't have happened to a nicer guy," Luffy said.

"Couldn't have happened to a nicer guy," Barrett said too, in almost perfect unison. The dog stared at him, eyes wide, but the cop didn't notice. "I guess that makes sense, Jasmine. But there's another thing. How'd you figure out that Lucille and Marshall saw something?"

"Instinct," Jasmine said. "I wish I had a better answer, but that's pretty much it. I had a strong feeling they were involved from the get go, and the feeling ratcheted up when I tried to interview Lucille and she acted so uncharacteristically mean. I knew something was up. But by the end, I was fairly certain they hadn't been the ones who killed Oliver, because they had no motive and... well, instinct. So that left one thing; they must have seen something."

Barrett nodded. "That's excellent, Jasmine. I wish the academy could teach instincts like yours, but it can't."

"Is there anything I didn't cover?" Jasmine asked.

"The tag from your backpack," said Barrett.

"Oh, yeah. Well, that one's easy to explain too."

"It is?"

"Of course. It fell off my bag, that's all. It must have been sitting there on the table or the bench after I talked to Oliver that day in the dining hall. He found it and picked it up. It was in his pocket, probably. Maybe the pocket of his shirt. He was wearing a pocketed shirt when he was found."

Barrett nodded. "Yeah, he was, wasn't he?"

"So we know how it got up there," Jasmine replied. "Oliver carried it with him. Maybe he didn't even know it was mine; he just treated it like a good luck talisman. Or maybe he did know it was mine."

"I don't follow," said Barrett.

"I mean, it could have been another of his insurance policies. Like leaving Sandra's ring with Keller. He might have known something bad would happen that night."

Barrett's face went pale. "God, I hope that's not it. That's sad."

"I don't know," said Jasmine. "There are some mysteries that can't be solved. Not by anyone. Is there anything else?"

"Yeah. Just one thing. That kid, Charles Dane. How does he factor in?"

"Marginally and tangentially," she replied with a grin. "I'm still trying to get to the bottom of that one."

"Will you let know what you find out?" he asked.

"Maybe."

"Well, a maybe's good enough for me. I think we're done for the day, Jasmine. Why don't you and Luffy go out and stretch your legs a bit?"

"Need a ride?" a familiar voice called.

Jasmine narrowed her eyes, shielding them with a hand, as she and Luffy stepped out of the station. The spring rains had given way to another wave of heat and sun, boiling the last of the dampness out of the ground.

Charles was there in the parking lot, waiting beside his parked car.

"Actually, I was going to take a walk," Jasmine said.

He shrugged. "I can join you, if you'll have me. Now that you know I'm not a murderer."

Jasmine laughed. "Sure. Come along."

They headed east away from the station, strolling through the bright, hot air out into the suburbs.

"It was you, wasn't it?" Jasmine asked.

"Hm?"

"You're the one who called the station that night and got me out."

"I'm afraid I have no idea what you're talking about."

"No? Come on, there's no use lying. Your family has weight around here. You could have swung it. You can tell me no, but you know me; I'll figure it out eventually."

"Yes," he said with a sigh. "I suppose you would. Fine, I admit it. I called in and gave Barrett a verbal thrashing that probably should have landed me in jail right next to you. But it worked."

"Why did you do it?" Jasmine asked.

He shrugged. "You're a friend, and I thought the idea of you killing Oliver was preposterous. And the idea of you sitting in jail didn't sit well. So I decided to do something about it."

"Yup," said Jasmine. "I'm sure that was it."

"What, you don't believe me? Is it so rare for people to take the initiative and do what's right in this world? I suppose it is. But that reflects well on me and poorly on the rest of humanity."

Jasmine grinned. "Keep telling yourself that."

Charles stared at her, clearly dumbfounded.

"He doesn't get it," Luffy said. "You'll have to guide him in."

"The ring," Jasmine said. "The favor you asked Alicia for. Breaking me out of jail. Hello?"

Charles narrowed his eyes... then suddenly burst out laughing.

"You thought you were the girl I had a crush on?" he asked.

"You're telling me I'm not?"

"Yes, I am telling you that. There's nothing the matter with you Jasmine, but you're not my type. I'm quite content to remain as friends."

"Then what...? Who...?"

"Christine Lackey," Charles said dreamily.

"Her?" Jasmine asked. She shrugged. "Well, fair enough. She is gorgeous. And nice."

"And smart," said Charles. "The most important thing."

"I'm smart too," Jasmine said.

"That you are. Almost frighteningly, in fact. I'm sorry, Jasmine. I don't know what else to say."

"So," said Jasmine, thinking back to a friend from Blackwood Cove. "This is how it feels from the other side. Ugly and embarrassing."

Charles laughed. "Don't be dramatic. I know you don't have those feelings for me either. Friends, yes?"

"Friends," she confirmed.

Luffy stepped up in between them, grinning up as he panted in the heat. "More friends! I love friends!"

"But that dog of yours still smells bad," Charles remarked.

"Ah, man, I can't wait to pee on your car again," Luffy added.

Jasmine laughed. Charles laughed with her. And they kept on walking for a little while longer, not thinking of or talking about anything in particular. But soon it would be time to start thinking again. Classes would start back up after a short break, in the wake of everything that had happened. Things would go back to normal, or as close to normal as they could get.

Jasmine just hoped no one else would die before she made it back home.

END OF BOOK 2

BOOK 3: After a dead body is discovered in the dusty stacks of the old library, the quiet seaside town of Blackwood Cove is once again plunged into a seemingly unsolvable case.